SHADOWS AT WAR

A NOVEL

KENNETH L. CAPPS

BQB

Virginia

Published in the United Sates by BQB Publishing
(an imprint of Boutique of Quality Books Publishing Company, Inc.)
www.bqbpublishing.com

978-1-939371-94-2 (p)
978-1-939371-95-9 (e)

Library of Congress Control Number: 2018940695

Book design by Robin Krauss, www.lindendesign.biz
Cover design by Ellis Dixon, www.ellisdixon.com

Other Books by Kenneth L. Capps

Forgiving Waters

Future Books in the Danger in the Shadows Series

Beyond the Shadows

CHAPTER ONE

April 2004

Young Scott Briggs thought he went unnoticed his first full day of boot camp as the drill instructors frantically ran back and forth screaming at the top of their lungs in order to herd the freshly shaven gaggle of boys into something that resembled a military formation. However, the fine eyes of his Marine Corps drill instructors did not miss the fact that Scott was far from ordinary as he stood with his face to the blistering South Carolina sun. His skin was no stranger to its punishing rays. It was dark, and the exposed patches not covered by his brand-new camouflage utility uniform shimmered with a fine glaze of sweat.

He stood just shy of five foot nine and never rested flat on his heels. To do so would keep him from reacting quickly if the need arose. His extraordinary balance and stance was placed in him by his heritage. His father and mother and their father and mother before them, all walked the decks and floorboards of small boats tossed about by the movement of wave and wind that showed no mercy to anyone caught flat-footed and unprepared.

His forearms were uncommonly thick and looked chiseled out of stone. His upper thighs split into two perfect bundles of muscle that flexed independently of one another depending on how much weight he burdened them with. His muscles were the product of a working man's life, not pumping iron under the fluorescent lights of a weight room. They came from leaning over the gunnels of small boats and hand pulling the burdened lines of full crab pots. These crab pots were not only full of blue crab but also the added overgrowth of barnacles. With each bow of his back as he heaved and pulled, his shoulders had grown wider and his waistline tighter.

———————

On his third night in the Marine Corps Recruit Depot at Parris Island, South Carolina, nineteen-year-old Scott Briggs felt he wasn't living up to his potential. He felt average in height and build compared to the other recruits in his platoon, but he was passionate about being a good Marine.

Each step he had made in the last three days kept running through his mind, and he couldn't sleep. He kept tossing and turning until his full bladder demanded attention. He carefully made his way through the silent barracks to the head. Stepping up to the urinal, he thought he heard something and stood quietly for a few moments, listening. He heard it again. It sounded like a mournful prayer coming from the shower room. With only moonlight shining through the large glass windows void of any shutter or shade, Briggs carefully followed the sound.

A recruit sat on the tile floor, the small blade of a Bic razor lying next to him in a growing pool of blood. The sobbing boy leaned against the far corner of the shower room holding a rosary in his hands, mumbling, "Please forgive me, Father, please . . ."

Before Briggs could comprehend what was happening, he instinctively pulled off his T-shirt and wrapped it around the boy's gashed wrists to stop the rapid flow of blood while yelling for the fire watch to wake the drill instructor on duty. An enormous amount of blood had pooled on the floor. Briggs had never seen so much blood, not even during his hunting adventures in the woods of the Outer Banks of North Carolina. He took a deep breath, tightly secured his T-shirt around the sobbing recruit's wrists, and held them elevated above the boy's head.

The senior drill instructor, Staff Sergeant K. L. Sholtz, rounded the corner. He flipped on the light switch, flooding the large room with bright light that reflected off the gleaming tiles and stainless steel surfaces. He quickly ordered the trailing fire watch to call for an ambulance. Sholtz stopped just short of the pool of blood that Briggs was kneeling in and carefully leaned over to check the boy's pulse at his neck.

"He still has a strong pulse. Briggs, you've done a fine job of stopping the bleeding. How long has he been like this?"

Briggs was surprised that his senior remembered his name and was astounded at Sholtz's calm and quiet demeanor. *He is human, after all,* Briggs thought. *Not spitting out orders or making me feel like the dirt under his boots, the way he normally does. He's just . . . talking to me.* Briggs considered the delicacy of that, the maturity it took for his senior to let go of the persona he needed for his job and calmly interact with him. The incident would stay with him for a long time.

"I'm not sure, sir. I've been here less than twenty seconds, sir," Briggs responded in a low voice.

"You're doing fine. Keep everything just like you have it, okay? The corpsman will be here shortly, and they will take over." Sholtz lightly placed his hand on Briggs's shoulder, then knelt and looked the injured recruit in the eye. "What's your name, son?"

The recruit responded with a fit of tears.

Sholtz quickly said, "Quiet now, it's okay. Everything's gonna be okay. Don't try to get up. You just stay still and let Briggs here take care of you."

The recruit nodded and started to shiver as he sobbed.

Sholtz had one more cautious question. "Why would you do such a thing, son?"

The recruit's words came pouring out amidst his sobs. "Because I can't make it. I want to go home. I just can't do it." He gulped in air. "It's just too hard," he stuttered. "But if I don't finish boot camp, I'll deeply disappoint my father, and I just can't do that to him. I'd rather die." The boy lapsed into uncontrollable sobbing as Briggs and his senior remained quietly by his side.

Briggs could not wrap his mind around the thought of suicide. It had never entered his thoughts, even when times were as bad as he thought they'd ever get. And he couldn't fathom why suicide would be better than disappointing someone, especially his father.

His father had died when he was fourteen. Briggs was not perfect as a kid, and he occasionally earned what his father called a "butt whippin'," but it was always brief and with a light hand. Never in his life had he heard a harsh word from him. Mostly his father told him he was proud of him. His father never missed an opportunity to congratulate him on the simplest job, even if it could have been done better. Briggs knew his father had just wanted him to learn and grow and prosper. They'd spent hours talking about life as they pulled crab pots or ran fishing nets in the early mornings in the tangled, shallow marshes of the Outer Banks. They were buddies and friends and talked about everything, even grown-up things—and that, more than anything, had made Briggs feel like a man, and made him the man he would become.

Looking at the young recruit, Briggs thought about how the boy's father would feel if he had died and the pain it would bring his family. Briggs himself had stood on the other side of death when his father passed and had mourned inconsolably when his father was buried.

Three corpsman arrived in an ambulance and quickly loaded the recruit onto a stretcher before racing away. The red-and-blue lights flashed through the windows. The senior drill instructor ordered the fire watch to get a hose and rinse out the shower before they turned out the lights. Then he turned to Briggs, told him he'd done a fine job and to clean up and hit the rack.

The next day, Briggs was given a new position as the squad leader of the fourth squad in his platoon of a hundred. He surprised himself at how easily he performed in a position of leadership. It was as if all the little things he'd learned in life finally fell into place. When he instructed his fellow recruits to follow the orders that were passed down to him from his drill instructors, he did it with a caring and considerate command. His fellow recruits did not think of him as bossy or insensitive and performed for him with respect.

Squad leader was a position that the majority of the mixed bag of young men—still pimple-faced and gangly—were far from prepared for. They flinched at the intensity, the anticipation of what their drill instructors would order. Survival in this new world called boot camp was the first order of business for the average recruit, not leadership or helping someone who was falling behind.

The platoon began with a hundred recruits. Attrition would dwindle the numbers to around seventy by graduation day.

CHAPTER TWO

May 2004

"Briggs, up on the quarterdeck," Sholtz barked.

The entire platoon stopped what they were doing and stood at attention, repeating the call from the duty hut in unison. "Sir, Recruit Briggs, aye-aye, sir."

Briggs scampered to his feet from behind the squad bay on the third deck of the building where he had been helping another recruit clean his weapon. All the windows were open, allowing the sweet summer breeze to flow through the hundred-foot-long room, which housed the entire platoon and its gear. The racks were two high and ran along each outside bulkhead with another set down the middle. Each rack had a dark-green plywood footlocker at its foot, and each rack was immaculately made with green blankets that had the letters "US" face up, dead center.

Briggs's heart beat rapidly as he sprinted toward the duty hut. Between the windows and the racks, the distance was only wide enough for two recruits to pass, and even at that they had to turn sideways in order to do so. However, one frantic recruit at a full run demanded the entire space in order to expedite his arrival at the command of his DI. Every recruit knew to "gangway" when someone was burning up the tile to answer a call from the duty hut. Anyone who did not was sure to get run over by someone making the hard blind turns a summoned recruit was taking. Briggs was up to a full head of steam when he swung into a hard left hand turn just before he made it past the last row of racks. One more turn to the right and he would arrive at the spot in the classroom in front of the duty hut.

While he ran, he recalled an event several weeks earlier, when the senior drill instructor was walking the quarterdeck during cleanup. He had sidled up to Briggs, who was sitting on the floor ironing his sheets. All the corners and folds were a perfect forty-five-degree angle, and the recruits took turns passing a hot iron down the line, plugging it in as they went so it would stay hot.

"That really makes the rack pop, doesn't it, Briggs?" Sholtz had said as he leaned over Briggs's shoulder from behind.

"Man, it sure does," Briggs replied as he passed the iron to the next waiting recruit. He was still sitting on the white tile floor of the barracks, which had been polished to a shine that reflected the streams of light flowing through the windows that ran the length of the squad bay on both sides. It even reflected the intense shock on Briggs's face when he realized he was speaking to his senior while sitting on the deck and hadn't started or ended his response with "sir." Worst of all, he'd referred to him as "man."

Oh God, I am so dead, Briggs thought to himself as he sprung to his feet.

When he pushed up from the deck and turned to face his senior, his head caught Sholtz just under the chin, knocking his senior's campaign cover—otherwise known as a Smokey—off his head.

Briggs immediately reached out to pick it up but had only brushed it with his fingertips when he was pushed backward onto his freshly made rack by Sholtz.

"Don't compound your mistake by making a bigger one, Briggs!" Sholtz shouted. "Don't ever touch a drill instructor's Smokey, you filthy, slimy turd. You have a long way to go before you earn that privilege."

Sholtz retrieved his Smokey and placed it back on his head before turning to confront Briggs, now standing at attention between the racks, shaking so badly he thought he would vibrate across the squad bay. He was certain he was in for Incentive Training.

His first experience with IT had been at the beginning of boot camp after the first and last time he dropped his rifle. After a run on a particularly hot afternoon, one of his junior drill instructors escorted him to what he called "a nice shady spot." In that nice shady spot, Briggs performed endless push-ups, turned onto his back to perform leg lifts, and flipped back again for more push-ups. For the next three minutes or so—an eternity in Briggs's mind—he ran in place with his rifle extended in front of his body at arm's length. Completely covered in sweat, he was ordered to hit the deck and roll repeatedly until dirt had clung to his face and arms and clothing, making him look like a human sugar cookie.

Since then, he'd tried his hardest to avoid being IT'd again, but with Sholtz glaring daggers at him, he feared the type of punishment he would have to endure for the egregious error of touching his senior's Smokey.

"I busted my ass to get this hat screwed on my head. It is sacred to me, and I hold this token of my accomplishments in very high regard. You're not worthy enough to touch it . . . ever! You have to earn the right to touch this hat, to own it, and to wear it. You're not even a Marine yet, you creepy little bag of dirt." Sholtz was only inches from his face, barking a rapid succession of words punctuated with an occasional bump from the brim of his hat on Briggs's forehead.

"So the next time you get tangled up in your own damn feet, have the common courtesy not to soil my Smokey with your filthy, undeserving hands."

"Sir, yes, sir!" Briggs snapped back.

With that, Sholtz had turned away and walked down the line of perfectly made racks without another word.

Briggs was horrified; he knew he would have to pay—somehow, some way. He just wasn't sure when or how.

The yell of his name from Sholtz and the platoon sounding off brought Briggs back to the present. His mind was so preoccupied with getting to the duty hut that he was only five steps away when he ran into another recruit standing at attention in the middle of the classroom surrounded by all his gear. The two of them fell to the deck in a tangle of bodies and sea bags. Briggs could feel Sholtz's presence before he heard the sarcastic bombast.

"Well, Briggs, I didn't know you would be so happy to see our new pickup recruit. If the two of you are finished sucking face and dry humping each other on my classroom deck, maybe you could show him to his rack."

Briggs jumped to his feet and kicked aside the sea bags in order to stand at attention. Before shouting a reply to his drill instructor's order, he reached down and pulled the new recruit to his feet alongside him.

"Sir, yes, sir!"

Though the man's height was impressive at six feet four, Briggs noticed that his arms were a little soft and he did not seem to possess the physical strength of a four-week recruit. Briggs wondered why this man had been brought to his attention. He had a feeling he was soon to find out.

Sholtz turned and walked back into the duty hut without saying another word.

Maybe I'll find out another day then.

"Come on, Recruit," Briggs said in a matter-of-fact way as he reached down and grabbed one of the bags, pointing the way toward the back.

The two of them walked between the racks to the far end of the squad bay. Once Briggs reached the last rack, he flung the bag onto the empty rack and turned to the man, extending his hand.

"My name is Scott Briggs," he said with a smile and a firm handshake. "I'm your squad leader. Welcome to our platoon."

The new recruit tossed his overstuffed sea bag onto the bed.

"Anthony Thornhill. Call me Tony. It's what all my friends call me."

Thornhill towered over Briggs's five-foot-eight frame. His hair was jet black, and his face was long and oval shaped with a tiny indentation in the center of his chin. His shoulders were square like a scarecrow. He had a broad, toothy smile and his eyes squinted tightly when he laughed. When Anthony stuck out his hand to shake Briggs's, his hand completely disappeared as Anthony's fingers wrapped completely around his.

"Here, let me get this foot locker open so we can start putting away your gear. Where's your rifle?" Briggs asked.

"I was never issued a rifle. I have been in the fat farm ever since I flunked the first phase physical fitness test."

"No kidding! I thought everyone was issued a rifle after the first few days here."

"I guess so, but I'm not sure. I've been here for forty-six days already."

"Holy crap! Boot camp is seventy-three days long, and we have just short of fifty days left in our training." Briggs squinted his eyes and did the math in his head. "That means you'll be stuck in this place a month longer than the rest of us. That's gotta blow big time," he said sympathetically.

"Yeah, but it's okay. I really don't mind."

"You've got to be kidding me! Isn't there something else you'd rather be doing than be stuck here getting devoured by sand fleas and constantly screamed at by drill instructors?"

"Of course there is, but I want to be a Marine. I want to be a Marine more than anything, so if this is what it takes, then I'll do it. I killed myself to pass the basic physical fitness test to get here, and I barely squeaked by. I was incredibly disappointed when I failed my first phase PFT, and I knew I would wind up in the fat farm, but I'm not giving up."

"Well, I'm glad you got guts because you'll need them. Our drill instructors don't cut any slack for anyone. And the worst part is they don't like to drop recruits. They feel that to lose a recruit is showing weakness on their part. Unfortunately, what that means for you is a lot of remedial workouts and exercise. You may have passed the basic PFT to get here, but one thing is for sure: you won't fail another one. It's my responsibility to make sure that you meet the expectations of our drill instructors. Failure here is not an option. The drill instructors would rather kill you, cut you into little pieces, and feed you to the alligators than allow you to embarrass them. They'll just claim that you ran off in the middle of the night and died out in the swamp."

Thornhill smiled and nodded. "I get it."

"So did you play football in high school?"

Thornhill shook his head.

"Basketball? Baseball?"

Again he shook his head.

"What sports did you play in high school?" Briggs asked as he grabbed the linens from the top rack. He held on one end of the fitted sheet as Thornhill stretched it out and started to make the bed.

"I didn't play any sports in high school. Don't get me wrong, I tried out for everything. I really wanted to play some sport—any sport—but, well, I guess you could say I'm just clumsy. That's kind of the reason why I'm here. I want to be a Marine, and for the first time in my life, I passed the tryouts, so they have to give me a chance. For the first time in my life, I'm on a team." Thornhill was smiling from ear to ear, showing his glistening white teeth. Briggs looked at him intently and realized that he possessed the most important thing there was for success: tenacity.

"Well, you're on our team now, buddy," Briggs said as he reached up to slap the big man's shoulder.

———

Thornhill and Briggs became close friends quickly. Over the next several weeks, Briggs helped him push his way through his clumsiness to physical perfection. Under the positive encouragement of Briggs, Thornhill was transformed. He turned out to be the strongest recruit in the entire company. During a companywide field day meet, he was able to do more push-ups and pull-ups than any other recruit in Echo Company. His floppy muscle had turned to granite, and his rolling belly had disappeared, replaced by a hard-packed V-shape from chest to waist.

Thornhill was there the day Briggs received "the letter"—the one Briggs knew would be coming. It was late one night a few weeks before graduation, and Thornhill and Briggs were both scheduled for the 0200 fire watch in the squad bay. Briggs was quiet, far away in his thoughts.

"Are you okay, Briggs?" Thornhill asked. "You've been kind of out there lately."

"Yeah. I mean, no," Briggs replied. Reaching into his pocket, he pulled out the crumpled envelope that contained the letter. He fumbled with it, switching it from one hand to the other, and then put it back into his pocket.

"It's my girlfriend, Anita; she's pretty much letting me go." Briggs's voice was just above a whisper. "She's the only girlfriend I've ever had, and she says she won't follow me to my next duty station when I leave boot camp."

Anita and Scott had known each other even before he could remember knowing her. She lived three miles away from his house down a road that was mostly shell and gravel. About the time he turned eight the road was paved. It was also made wider and into two lanes. On the old road one would have to give way to any approaching vehicle and ease over into the tall grasses that came up past the knee. Road maintenance at the far edge of Carteret County in the tiny town of Gloucester, North Carolina, was always at the bottom of the list. However, treacherous roads and tall grass that harbored snakes and other critters that scared the daylights out of a less amorous heart were no deterrent for Anita and Scott.

Their parents took turns babysitting them from when they were toddlers until they no longer needed a babysitter. The road and a handful of residents that occupied the scattered houses they passed coming and going witnessed their blossoming love. From being driven by their parents up to driving their own cars their love grew as did the road they traveled. If a bike tire succumbed to the punishing gravel of the road, they would walk the rest of the way without complaining. Asking someone to give them a ride might mean they would have to wait in order to make their travel arrangements. It was faster to walk, a walk that always turned into a jog.

When Scott got his first boat, Anita's dock was his first stop. It was only a one-mile paddle from his dock to hers. And when he purchased his first outboard, the trip only took four minutes. Most of the time was spent tying up and untying the twelve-foot Downeaster flat bottom boat he and his father had built. They had doubled the thickness of the transom with a single sheet of mahogany his father had been saving for what he described as "something special." How fortuitous for Scott. The 1959 Johnson Super Seahorse only produced 10 hp, but the light wooden Downeaster skipped over the choppy water with ease as he made his way back and forth to Anita's dock. They were everything to each other and nothing kept them apart.

"So were the two of you going to get married?"

"Not yet, at least—and now probably not ever. But I still want to marry her," Briggs replied in a fading voice.

"That must be the picture."

"What?"

"The picture you have taped inside your knowledge book," Thornhill said. "I've seen it a few times just never bothered you about it because you didn't volunteer to show it to me or explain who it was. For all I know it could have been your sister."

"What!" Briggs gave Thornhill a startled look.

"Hey, hey, don't get pissed, dude. If you have a freak thing going on with your sister, who am I to say you're wrong?"

"What are you talking about?" Briggs was more confused than startled now.

"I've seen the picture in your notebook. Hell, if my sister were that hot I might be tempted to go to the dark side too." Thornhill gave Briggs a sideways look and then a toothy grin.

"Stop that shit! You know that's not my sister." Briggs gave Thornhill a shove. They broke into a chuckle.

"So let me see the picture." Thornhill held out his hand.

Briggs removed the small green 4" × 5½" binder from the Cammy pocket of his trousers and opened it to reveal Anita's picture taped to the inside front cover. She was standing at the end of a boat dock in a bikini that left nothing to the imagination. A Corona bottle with a lime slightly tucked in at the neck dangled from her left hand. Condensation distorted the bottle's label, and small drops sparkled as they fell to the deck below. The vibrant rays of the setting sun behind her reflected off the water like broken glass.

She was so evenly tanned it looked sprayed on. Her legs and

arms were long and slender, and long blonde hair blew around her face in the slight breeze coming off the Bay. The flash of the camera highlighted her firm, high cheekbones and green eyes as well as the glistening beads of perspiration on her chest and cleavage. She wore no makeup; it wasn't necessary for such a vibrant beauty.

"She sounds like she's very special."

Briggs leaned against the wall behind him. "We've been boyfriend and girlfriend since grade school. As we got older, it turned to love and everyone in my hometown was certain it was forever love." Briggs's eyes were sad as he continued. "But things change. When I was fourteen, my dad was diagnosed with cancer; the doctors told us that there was nothing we could do because the cancer was advanced and inoperable."

Thornhill remained silent but placed his hand on Briggs's shoulder in a compassionate way.

"I was there every step of the way as, in just a few months, he regressed from walking with a cane, to sitting in a wheelchair, and then being confined to a hospital bed." Briggs took a deep breath. "It was a terrible time for my family, but we supported each other, and Anita was there for me every step of the way."

"I'm so sorry, man. That must have been horrible."

"It changed me, Tony." Briggs dropped his head and was quiet for several minutes before looking up. "I couldn't stay there after that. The Outer Banks were no longer the same. Everywhere I looked there were memories of my father, and it was just too much. But Anita didn't understand. She had no intention of leaving the area or Marshallberg. She said that life there gave her comfort and peace, and she was surrounded by the supportive relationships that would carry her into old age. We had quite a spat about it, and she was sure I'd change my mind."

"But you didn't?"

Briggs shook his head. "I turned eighteen, joined the Marine Corps, and left for boot camp. I've sent letters to my mom and Anita every week. At first, Anita's replies came quickly, but they've been coming less frequently and the tone hasn't been the same."

A huge sigh escaped from Briggs. "Her last letter said she wouldn't be at boot camp graduation. But I've kept writing, trying to change her mind."

"That's real hard, man. Is she the only girl you've ever been with?"

Briggs nodded, then shook his head. "Wait, what do you mean by 'been with'? She's the only girlfriend I have ever had, and if 'been with' means 'had sex with' . . . well, no."

Thornhill's eyes went wide. "Wait a minute. You've never had sex with her or any girl? Like, you're a virgin?" He held up his hands. "I'm not trying to bust your chops or anything. It's just . . . surprising is all."

"No, Tony, I've never had sex with her or any other girl. She is the one—I mean the one, the one I'm supposed to be with the rest of my life. Even after how much I changed after my dad died, my love for her only grew. I know we need to be together right down to my soul." Briggs took a few steps away from Thornhill into the darkness of the squad bay.

"Hold on a minute. The math just doesn't add up here. All my life I was the big, dumb, fat, clumsy kid, and I've been laid more than once. And you, Mister Shine, you've been saving yourself for this girl. That's a big deal, dude." Thornhill caught up to Briggs and placed his arm around his shoulder in a sympathetic gesture.

"Thanks," Briggs said in a hollow voice.

"Listen, on graduation day, my entire family's coming down here from New Jersey. I'll introduce you to my sister. She's ugly as hell, but easy. You can get that virginity thing out of the way quick, and it will change your whole perspective, brother."

Briggs chuckled and swatted Thornhill on the arm. "Er, thanks but no thanks."

Thornhill smiled. "You know I'd do anything in the world for you, brother. All you have to do is ask," he said with his mischievous grin so wide it lit up the darkened squad bay.

"I know you would, man. I just wish I knew what that 'anything' was."

CHAPTER THREE

June 2004

The end of boot camp was just two days away, and the recruits no longer had to sound off or scurry about like roaches fleeing a blinding light in order to impress or please their drill instructors. They had already accomplished that and so much more.

Days had quickly turned into weeks and weeks into months and now boot camp and all its exhausting and chaotic rituals was coming to an end. Every recruit in Platoon 2036 had metamorphosed into a Marine by definition, if not by name. They were strong and bronzed from the sun, with chiseled jaws and long lines of muscle in their legs and backs. Most importantly, they were confident. The recruits walked with purpose. They were called Marines at this point in their training by everyone save one—their senior.

Staff Sgt. Sholtz emerged from the duty hut and adjusted his Smokey so that it tilted down low over his brow. "Briggs!" Sholtz commanded.

Briggs stopped in his tracks and sprinted to the front of the duty hut, "Recruit Briggs reporting as ordered, sir," Briggs said as he stopped in front of Sholtz.

"Do you know where DI school is?" Sholtz asked.

"Yes, sir."

"Master Gunnery Sergeant Hager is in charge of the DI school, and he would like to see you at his office."

A concerned look passed over Briggs's face.

"He served with your father in Vietnam, and he wishes to speak with you."

"Now, sir?" Briggs asked.

"He said at your pleasure, which means he has a great deal of respect for you, Briggs. He is giving you the privilege of inconveniencing him. Top is a good man, so don't keep him waiting."

Briggs started to speak, but Sholtz stopped him. "It's a good thing, son. He is proud of you and wants to tell you so himself."

Now Briggs was totally confused. His presence had been requested by a high-ranking Marine with more stripes on his sleeve than anyone on the base, and he was allowing a lowly recruit to take his time in getting there. Not to mention the fact that his senior drill instructor had just called him "son."

Briggs collected himself and stopped off in the head in order to wash his hands and face. He checked his reflection in the mirror, adjusted his uniform, and made a dash effort to brush polish his boots before running out the back of the squad bay and down the back ladder well. This was the shortest distance to the DI school barracks.

He found himself running at double time and made himself slow to a conservative quick march in order to not arrive sweaty. The relentless South Carolina sun glaring down on Parris Island was daunting and favored no one, especially young wannabe Marines who had yet to earn the title.

"Sir, Recruit Briggs reporting as ordered, sir," Briggs announced as he stepped in front of the duty desk just inside the open hall.

It was after hours and turning dark, but beyond the door of the barracks, the echoes of the DI school candidates rang like music throughout the buildings. They recited running chants and drill movements. They were all about the place—passageways, heads, and outlying corridors. They huddled together in small groups, honing to perfection the skills a Marine Corps drill instructor must possess. Briggs felt honored and privileged to stand in such a hallowed place, where the best of the best diligently sacrificed their own personal wants to tread a path that would lead them to the most paramount position, teacher of Marines.

"You're Briggs?"

"Yes, sir."

The duty sergeant stood from his desk and motioned for Briggs to follow him to the office of Master Gunnery Sergeant Hager. Hager thanked the duty sergeant who closed the door behind him. Hager motioned to Briggs to take a seat in an oversized leather chair. The walls were covered with pictures of campaigns that Hager had been involved in. His desk was enormous with ornate carvings in the wood on all four corners and the Marine Corps emblem carved in the center of it.

Briggs felt incredibly awestruck and incredibly confused. He still had no idea what this was all about.

Finally, Hager spoke. "I suppose you're wondering what this little meeting is all about." Briggs started to spring to his feet to respond, but Hager raised his hand. "No, it's not that kind of meeting, son. This is something very special, and I want you to sit there and relax. You can speak to me while you're seated. Boot camp is over."

"Yes, sir, but—"

"Call me Top, son. Everyone calls me Top. 'Top' is a term used for the top sergeant and is a respectful term that I embrace. What's more, the only reason I am able to be called that is because of your father."

Hager sat on the corner of his desk and crossed his thick, strong arms, smiling at Briggs with warm, dark eyes. Though not big in stature, his presence was massive, his dark skin smooth over an honest face that put Briggs at ease. The ribbons above Hager's left breast pocket were stacked five high and five across. Above them were the most coveted of all awards—gold jump wings and a silver scuba mask—the true mark of a Recon Marine. Briggs had never seen so many ribbons on one shirt and could not help but stare at them.

Hager uncrossed his arms, walked across the room, and picked up a picture on the shelf. "Recognize this guy?" Hager asked as he handed the photo to Briggs.

"That's my father," Briggs replied with a surprised smile. "I thought I had seen all of his pictures."

"Do you recognize the man to his left?"

"No, sir . . . wait, that's you."

"That's right. A lot younger and a lot better looking, but you're right, that's me."

Hager walked over and sat in the chair across from Briggs.

"Son," he looked into Briggs's eyes, "I'm going to tell you a story that I've been rehearsing in my head ever since I learned that the son of Corporal Lee Briggs was on his way to Parris Island."

He leaned forward in his chair as his eyes looked past Briggs. "It was 1966 and your father, several other Marines, and I were advancing on a position adjacent to a hillside that was infested with North Vietnamese. Our squad was being attacked from several different directions and mortar and automatic weapon fire rained down on us from unknown sources." His voice trailed off as he was transported to the past.

"There was a brief lull in the attack that lasted no more than thirty seconds. Suddenly, North Vietnamese soldiers emerged from the jungle, lunging and shooting." He paused and looked directly at Briggs. "Your father was at the very end of our string of Marines as we worked our way through the jungle. When he saw his fellow Marines being attacked, he rushed forward, firing his weapon and screaming like a madman." His eyes glistened with the memory.

"I'll spare you all the gory details and the war-story rhetoric, but in the end, your father saved the lives of many men in our platoon. I don't know if you've read the award for his Medal of Honor yourself. Half of it is bullshit, but the fact is, if it were not for your father, I would not be here today. I watched him run with his usual mastery, shooting, reloading, and picking up the weapons of the dead, using them instead of reloading his own to save time. I thought to myself: 'This guy is Superman.'

"A third or fourth mortar landed behind me, and I got shrapnel in both my knees. I could still return fire and fight, but I could not move—not even an inch. Your father shot the first Vietcong who walked up behind me to put a bullet in my head, and then he shot another. We were pinned down all over the place. In between the smoke and the weapons fire, your father was everywhere—moving, shifting, and shooting. Unbelievably, he never hit the ground. After spending two more tours in that hellhole, what I witnessed in your father was the most impressive combat expertise I have ever seen. Your father was a true warrior."

Hager reached across from his chair and extended his hand to Briggs. "Congratulations, Marine."

Briggs beamed as he reached out and firmly clasped his hand in Hager's palm.

"I know you've been called a Marine after you passed your Crucible. That's just a bunch of feel-good, warm-and-fuzzy trash the grade types came up with when the company commanders started getting jealous when they found out they would never wear a Smokey." The grin on Hager's face was deep and mischievous. "Trust me, it doesn't mean shit until you've been called a Marine by a Marine who has been there."

Briggs assumed "been there" meant having been in combat, which made a lot of sense.

"I bet Sholtz hasn't called you a Marine yet. He's old school like me. Even though he hasn't been around that long, he still holds on to the true values of the Corps." He shifted his weight from one side to the other, and the dark maroon-colored leather squeaked as it stretched. "I wanted to be the first, because I owe your father an incredible debt that I will never be able to repay. And I suspect the acorn doesn't fall far from the tree."

Hager stood, walked over to the other end of his desk, and opened one of the mahogany drawers. He removed a set of Eagle, Globe, and Anchor emblems, which he handed to Briggs.

"It would be an honor if you would wear these on your uniform. A small token of my gratitude, which I hope you cherish, as I have."

Briggs blinked, awestruck. "Thank you, sir. This means so much to me, and I will indeed cherish them. Without a doubt." He gazed at the emblems in his upturned palms and warm memories of his father and his family washed over him, accompanied by a whisper of sadness because his father wasn't alive to enjoy this experience with him.

A thought trickled through his mind, and he looked into Hager's eyes. "It was my mother who let you know I was coming to Parris Island, wasn't it?"

"Yes, she gave me a call and told me you were on your way down here. It was nothing more than that, just a phone call. After Vietnam, your father got out of the Marine Corps, but I stayed. We kept in touch, but it was a once-a-year thing. I was even at your house once on the Outer Banks before . . ." Hager paused.

Before your father died, Briggs thought.

"You weren't there at the time. I think you were out fishing or something," Hager recovered quickly.

He smiled as he returned his attention to the conversation. "She is your mother and she gets to do things like that, whether you like it or not."

"I understand, sir."

"Well, I guess I will see you and your family this Friday at graduation." Hager stood and held out his hand. "Then I'll get a chance to shake your hand in public and we'll have a proper introduction." With that, Hager slapped him on the arm and said, "I'm proud of you, Scott."

The irony of the statement didn't miss Briggs. He knew his father would have said the same thing.

The night before graduation Sholtz quietly called his men to the quarterdeck and asked them to gather round. After spending weeks under Sholtz's command, Briggs recognized this was not an order, not a command, but a request to a group he respected. The platoon stood shoulder to shoulder in a tight formation with just enough room between them to sit cross-legged on the deck if told.

"At ease, at ease," Sholtz began as he motioned his hands down in a gentle pushing motion. Briggs and the entire platoon stood at ease. "I want to start by saying thank you for voluntarily enlisting into the world's finest fighting force, the United States Marine Corps, and coming here to keep me entertained these last seventy-three days."

The platoon broke into laughter, which slowly tapered off as Sholtz held up his hand to continue his speech.

"I am proud of you. Each and every one of you came here knowing that you are about to step into harm's way. For two hundred twenty-nine years, brave men like you have stepped forward to join a brotherhood that stands against tyranny, for justice, and with pride—a gesture of selflessness, which holds great honor. It's been tough on you, I know. It was tough on me when I was in your boots, and that is now something we share in common. This is my Marine Corps, and you can't come in unless you measure up, unless you pass the test—or this would just be daycare."

Laughter broke out again as Briggs and the entire platoon stood a little taller at Sholtz's words. Sholtz extended his arms and pointed at the young faces before him in sweeping motions. "And thanks to all of you for allowing me the joy of passing on the tradition of my Marine Corps to you.

"You now all share two birthdays that will define you for the rest of your life. November 10, 1775, the birthday of your Corps, and June 18, 2004, the day you officially become Marines. But tonight, as you spend your very last night together as a platoon, before you close your eyes, remember this place and what you have learned. The sound of your boots striking the ground in unison as one, like thunder."

His voice rose to a climax as he lifted his chin, clenched his fists, and closed his eyes. The platoon roared in response to his obvious emotion. Slowly, the cheers of the platoon faded and calmed, but Sholtz was still bathing in the moment as he lowered his chin and opened his eyes.

"No matter if you stay in for one more day or retire after thirty years, you are a Marine forever. Take what you have learned here and use it to better your lives."

The platoon soaked in every word and could barely contain their emotions at his candid, fatherly words. They patted each other on the backs and let out the occasional *oorah*. All around Briggs, the recruits' normally stone-faced expressions softened as they smiled in satisfaction at this, their moment. More of that was to come tomorrow.

"It is my honor to embrace you as my brothers—as Marines."

At the completion of Sholtz's speech, the squad bay erupted into an explosion of applause that blasted through the windows and reverberated off the bulkheads louder than thunder, louder than combat. It continued while Sholtz waded his way through the crowd of smiling faces to shake the hand of Briggs and every Marine in his platoon. He was proud of them all.

The euphoria lasted well after lights-out as the fledgling Marines milled about, talking and spending just a few more moments, trying to cut the edge of the excitement enough to fall asleep.

CHAPTER FOUR

June 18, 2004

The drive home from Parris Island to the tiny town of Gloucester, North Carolina, was a little over eight hours. During the drive Briggs realized that to his family and friends, he was Scott, the boy who grew up on the Outer Banks and loved fishing and being on the water. For everyone who knew him as a Marine, he was Briggs. He felt like a man with two identities, two lives—and he was okay with that. In fact, the two identities fit him well.

Scott was glad to be going home after the rigors of boot camp. Gloucester was just a little stretch of sand held together by pine trees, live oak roots, and sea oats perched atop a clay bed. It had defied hurricanes and brought forth generations of good folk who made their living from the marshes and shallows behind the protection of the Outer Banks, a two-hundred-mile string of barrier islands along the North Carolina coast. His treasured hometown existed at the mercy of the Outer Banks, which stood between the strong surf of the Atlantic and the mainland. Situated between two massive bays and the Pamlico Sound, Gloucester was his world, his joy, and all he'd ever wanted—until his father died.

Even now, the hunger to fish and be a part of the heritage of the Outer Bank was embedded in every aspect of his life. This was his home, and he took from the waters what would sustain him and his family.

More importantly, he felt like a steward of this spectacular place—"a keeper of the sand," his father had called it. His father had told him that even though a hurricane and the mighty hand of Mother Nature could sculpt the Outer Banks and change it as it saw fit, it was a man's responsibility to maintain a balance that benefited all. Scott understood that. He recognized that each little thing, no matter how miniscule it seemed, was the reason something else thrived, each giving life to the other. Scott never looked at anything in an ordinary way.

Time flew by with the markers on the side of the road. Scott, his mom, his sister Michelle, and her husband Mike all took turns driving the minivan as Briggs regaled them with stories about how his drill instructors went from scaring the hell out of him to relying on him to help lead the platoon.

The van was crowded with luggage and conversation; however, nothing took up more room than the elephant that grew with each passing mile. No one mentioned Anita, and Scott was afraid to ask. His biggest fear was that she had met someone and was lost to him forever. He wanted to know, yet he didn't.

Finally, the wanting to know won out and he blurted, "How is she doing?"

A collective silence fell so quickly that for the first time they noticed the car radio was on. His mother, Alma, turned down the volume to increase the silence, then reluctantly told him that Anita was seeing someone else. He was the son of a wealthy investment company owner who was buying up waterfront property wherever it was available.

"They even made an offer on the fish house, Scott," Michelle said, trying to divert the conversation. "It's a tempting offer," she added when he didn't respond. Michelle and her husband owned a fish house, one of the few remaining businesses on the water's edge, where they sold bait and purchased fish and crab from the local fishermen. They also sold bulk-cleaned fish that were trucked out daily to several restaurants in the area.

At the mention of Anita's new love interest, Scott felt his stomach knot up. Silence returned to the group. No one said another word until Scott resumed his boot camp stories as if Anita had never been mentioned.

But the damage was done. Scott had known it would hurt when his biggest fears were confirmed; he just wasn't prepared to be trapped in such a small space when he found out, unable to escape the stinging echo of the truth. If he were home, he could have picked up a rod and reel, walked across the backyard, and jumped into his boat. The sound of the outboard running would have soothed the pain, and the splashing water on the hull would have drowned out the sound of his heart breaking.

They arrived home late that night and piled out of the van, stretching and yawning. Those who'd slept for the last hour of the drive retrieved everyone's belongings while the others stumbled into the house, exhausted.

━━━◆━━━

The next morning, Scott was the first to rise. The habits of boot camp were hard to break, and the joy of greeting the sunrise as it flooded the morning air with color was worth the effort. He was walking across the dew-covered grass when he heard her voice.

"Welcome home."

Scott turned to see Anita standing by the side of the house. She wore short blue-jean cutoffs and a button-up shirt. The top two buttons were undone, giving him an enticing view of her freckled, tanned chest. Scott stood frozen, entranced by her beauty. Her bike leaned against a tree behind her—she'd ridden her bike the three miles from her house, the same ride she'd made every day during grade school to get on the bus with him until he got his first car and drove them to school.

"It's good to see you," Scott said, but he did not approach her. He studied her as she slowly moved toward him, stopping just beyond a hug's length away.

"I like the haircut." She giggled nervously. "It looks good."

"Yeah, I've gotten used to it. Are you okay?" he asked, suddenly feeling shy.

She shook her head lightly as tears welled up in her eyes. She broke from her position and dashed the short distance into his arms. She buried her face in his chest and mumbled, "I miss you so much."

She felt as soft as a pillow as he wrapped his arms around her and squeezed. Her long blonde hair smelled of jasmine and fresh linen. He drew in a deep breath, indulging himself in her scent, her touch. They had never been apart for more than a week since they were eight years old, and seventy-three days had just passed without them seeing each other. She held him tightly and softly sobbed. For an instant he thought everything was going to be all right, that she had changed her mind and was going to go with him, be with him wherever he went. Afraid to speak, he just hung on and hoped. The choice was all hers, of course, and he would have to live with it, no matter what her decision was. But the moment felt good, so he held on and pretended that his dreams would come true.

"I'm sorry. I'm so sorry."

He felt her embrace start to slip ever so slightly, so he did the same.

"I'm so sorry, Scott." She slid from his arms and turned so he could not see her face. She broke away from him and ran, her hair shimmering behind her in the rays of the sun as it rose over the Outer Banks, bouncing off the water in brilliant yellows and oranges.

Unlike the rising sun, his moment of bliss disappeared, the joy in his heart and head shutting down like the slam of a door.

He heard the sound of her bike as she peddled down the shell driveway. His heart was crushed. The only remnants of their relationship now were his tear-soaked T-shirt where her face had pressed against his chest.

The rest of his leave went by in a blur as he pretended everything was okay. But he was breaking on the inside as he tried to accept the fact that Anita was no longer a part of his life.

In July, he returned to duty and was assigned to the 2nd Marine Division, 2nd Battalion, 8th Marine Regiment in Camp Lejeune, North Carolina, only a few hours from his home.

When he was able to go home, he had to force himself to stop looking for Anita. It was difficult to do in such a small town. Instead, he would go fishing.

Fishing was like therapy for Scott. He would lose himself in the tangled backwaters of the islands. Some weekends, he would bring home one of the guys from the base who were thankful for the opportunity to be away from the lonely quiet of an empty barracks. They would camp out under the stars of the windswept beaches, feasting on the day's catch of crab, flounder, and the occasional cast net full of shrimp.

One evening, after dinner, Scott and his family settled onto the back porch with cold beers, watching the setting sun fading into the water. Wade, who was his Marine guest for the weekend, asked, "How could you ever want to leave a place like this, Scott?"

"I don't know," he replied. "I guess it's like having lobster every night of your life. It becomes so familiar that you don't appreciate it as much as you should." That was the convenient answer; the truth was far more painful to talk about.

Wade hoisted his drink and laughed. "Yeah, I sure would like to get tired of this."

Scott let out a sigh, holding back his mixed feelings about being home.

———————◆———————

Over the next year, the months of military training that followed were a welcome distraction, keeping him from thinking about Anita. Marine combat training, school of infantry training, and desert training at Twentynine Palms Base, California, occupied his life. The trips home became less frequent as Briggs's combat training continued and progressed. Duty weekends and additional desert training at Twentynine Palms also kept him away for longer periods of time. In a way it made things easier because he didn't have to worry about running into Anita. When he did go home, even though his friends didn't mean to bring up the subject, news would inevitably reach his ears about Anita and her now-fiancé. Scott tried to let the comments roll off his back each time—his friends and family meant no harm. It was a small town with small-town gossip. The subject was premium fare.

The gut punch came the day he found out that Anita had married and moved to Morehead, North Carolina, a half hour from Gloucester. Because they were so close, now there was a good chance he would not only run into Anita but into the newlyweds—double the agony.

When Scott's order came for Iraq, he was almost relieved to be able to put more distance between him and his past—behind him and Anita.

CHAPTER FIVE

June 2005

Iraq was cold the morning of his first patrol. Briggs was the newbie, the fish, the one most likely to die first because he was as green as a brand-new sea bag, void of discolorations and scars from journeys traveled. Everyone gave him a wide berth. But as the patrol went on through the day, the more experienced Marines could see that he fit in; maybe he was green, but he was instinctively smart. He rarely spoke and flawlessly executed and responded to every hand signal. Mostly he observed, taking in the activity around him, both obvious and subtle, learning, turning things over in his mind, cultivating his understanding. His footfalls light and balanced, he moved phantom-like, soundless and purposeful. He was aware of his proximity to cover, and he knew to keep the sun and shadows in his favor. Briggs's gear, which would normally rattle as he moved, was rigged to his body as if it were no more than a loose-fitting shirt, making no sound and allowing him the freedom of movement. Outwardly Briggs had a calm demeanor, but underneath he was a coiled spring, ready to take action.

Marine Lieutenant Colonel Check was with them this morning. Check was combat-experienced with three Purple Hearts. He was part of an elite team of Marines known as Force Recon, based on the USS *Nassau*. As such, Check was privileged to move among the battalion as he saw fit, to gather intelligence and an overall sense of the area. If word came from Lt. Col. Check, it was law, and a compliment from him could elevate a Marine to a highly respected position among his peers.

"Kid's impressive," Briggs overheard Check remark to the squad leader, Shannon Corr, who nodded as he stamped out a cigarette under his boot.

Corr squinted, exhaling smoke between his teeth. "Yes, sir."

Check's words stayed with Briggs as they patrolled the streets, looking left, looking right, zigzagging back and forth, trading off positions. The Marines noticed a slight change in the atmosphere, in the activity on the streets. The children who would usually come out to run alongside them until they showered them with handfuls of candy had mysteriously disappeared. Also gone were the kids who would occasionally kick a soccer ball in their direction, anxiously hoping for a return volley. As the temperature started to change, windows that should have been open to allow in the cooler breeze were now barely cracked or shut altogether. The squad watched as shop doors banged shut followed by the scrape of the locks and bolts.

The hair on Briggs's neck started to twitch and itch. The men instinctively moved closer to the buildings in order to avoid dangers that might come from above. Briggs noticed a shadow dart across the edge of the street.

Then he felt the blast over his left shoulder—a grenade or land mine. There was cover to his right, but another Marine was well on his way to claiming the small space between two brick embankments. He quickly surveyed his other options and found a doorway just two long strides away. Of course, two strides in a hot firefight was the equivalent of a million miles. Still, he did not falter. The sounds of rifle rounds and explosions all around him were confusing, deafening, and exhilarating all bundled into one overwhelmingly powerful emotion. Nothing in his training could be compared to this very moment when it all got real. One second he could hear everything and then intertwined with the pressure and blinding glow of an explosion, pure silence hung in the air surrounded by smoke and the smell of gunpowder. *Go.*

Another explosion ignited to his left, like a thunderclap at his heels, delivering a hot flash to his cheek an instant after he felt the pressure from the blast. He was only a motion into his first stride to reach the doorway when an intense pain hastened him along, burning its way through his left side.

I'm hit!

The words echoed through his mind, but there was no emotion attached to that reality. He simply reacted to the situation. His sole focus was on the mission—to survive, fight, and protect.

Small arms fire from AK-47s riddled the buildings and street. The rounds ricocheted off the walls and sidewalks, buzzing as they whizzed around his head. The noise seemed to come from everywhere—high, low, sideways. It scared the living hell out of Briggs.

An immense *CRACK!* was the next sound he heard. He stumbled and hit the pavement, and pain shot up his left leg. Something had bounced off of the concrete and crashed into his thigh. He quickly regained his balance. He put his head down and bolted in the direction of the doorway at full speed violently swinging his arms and weapon. Just one more step and he would be at the doorway. It was all happening so fast.

One more step and I'll be safe. I'll return fire. Provide cover. I'll be fine. I'll be fine. I'll be fine. Just one more step.

He took one more step.

A loud thud brought water to his eyes. His helmet slid down over his nose.

"Damn it!" Briggs yelled at the top of his lungs, landing on his right foot just in front of the doorway.

Then he heard another noise—a familiar noise, but one he

couldn't immediately place. With it came intense, ripping pain as a bullet entered his left forearm and his rifle slipped from his grip. He held back the urge to vomit. *No time,* he thought as he focused his attention on retrieving his weapon that had fallen on the concrete beside him. Just behind him, there was another explosion, impossibly bigger than the one that had started all this.

He was now inside the building, blinded by the sudden lack of harsh desert sunlight, but he sensed . . . something.

"What the hell?" he said, startled by a heavy weight hitting his helmet—a falling timber board?—and knocking his helmet to skitter on the ground. Something else punched him in the middle of his chest. "Shit!" He reached out into the darkness to balance himself on whatever he could get his hands on.

Unfortunately, it was the hot barrel of an AK-47, the enemy still on the other end.

Immediately, Briggs understood the events of the last fifteen seconds.

He had been shot several times. The first round hit his helmet, dropping it down over his eyes so he couldn't see the muzzle flash of the AK. The second went clean through his left forearm, causing him to drop his rifle. The familiar sound had been his skin and shirt sleeve stretching to the point where it snapped like the sound of a round passing through a target when pulling butts on the rifle range. The third round struck him directly in the hard plate of his flak jacket, as did the fourth.

Target practice.

Shit on that.

With this brief assessment of the chain of events, Briggs's instincts ignored the fear and pain and brought him back to strategy for survival. Using his forward momentum from his staggering run and the blast, he bear-hugged the enemy using the strength of his upper arms to compensate for his injured left forearm. The man lost his weapon at the impact, the AK-47 flying to the side.

The force of the next blast outside sent the two of them, still entwined in a life-or-death grip, tumbling down a set of stairs, sending shards of pain through his injured arm. Ignoring the pain, Briggs knew this was a rare stroke of luck for his survival—as long as there were no other weapons on the man. He would have to release one of his hands in order to pull his Ka-Bar from the strap on his suspenders. He prayed the combat knife was still there and that his retrieval of the weapon would be smooth.

His wounds were bleeding and the loss of blood would make him weak. The man he was fighting in the pitch dark of the basement seemed uninjured and big, wearing only a cartridge belt and chest strap, which scratched unmercifully at Briggs's chin.

Luckily for Briggs he was on top during the fall. The man's back slammed into the floor and Briggs felt the air blast out of his mouth as he collided with the concrete. This was his chance to retrieve his knife.

Briggs released his right-hand grip on the enemy.

As soon as he did, the man squirmed and rolled over onto his belly and tried to scramble away. In a single motion, Briggs flipped the safety on his knife holster and drew. He held on to the man's cartridge belt with his injured left hand, which burned like hellfire.

One chance, he thought. *It won't be clean, but it's all I got.*

He flipped his grip on the butt of the knife, and with a violent downward thrust, he struck. The Ka-Bar pierced the man's cartridge belt and through the man's body, halting at the concrete floor. Using the knife as leverage, Briggs pulled himself up. As he was regaining his balance, the knife slipped and then came to an abrupt stop at the man's hip bone, slicing open the man's back just below his ribs. The man's screams echoed against the concrete walls, the first time Briggs had heard him make a sound. The man reached around with his right hand to where the knife had slashed open his back.

The battle outside raged on.

Briggs could hear numerous explosions and small arms fire, but they were not as loud as they should have been—more like thuds and thumps vibrating the walls and shaking the dirt from the rafters.

Should be louder. And why is it so dark?

Briggs's moment of reflection cost him. The man managed to roll over onto his back and grip Briggs's throat in two meaty hands. Pushing his thumbs deep into Briggs's Adam's apple, he screamed in Arabic as he shook him back and forth. His murderous cries, along with his spit and the smell of his breath, assaulted Briggs's eyes, mouth, and nose.

Briggs still had the Ka-Bar firmly clenched in his bloody right hand. Forcing his hand between them, he drew it across the man's abdomen, high enough to miss the web belt and breach the tender belly. He sliced with little effort, unimpeded by the soft flesh. Briggs pushed the man backward, trying to break the stranglehold, all the while firmly gripping the Ka-Bar. His arm slipped completely through the enemy's torso, feeling the heat of the man's innards. The man went into an uncontrollable convulsion, finally loosening his grip on Briggs's neck.

Briggs gasped in a breath through his bruised throat, losing the Ka-Bar to the gore of the man's ribcage as the now mortally wounded man squirmed onto his belly and once again started to crawl away. This time, however, he had little strength left, and his screams dwindled to sobs.

The sense of urgency passed.

Unable to retrieve the Ka-Bar to finish the job, Briggs took a deep breath and crawled onto the man's back. Slipping his aching left arm under the man's left armpit and his right arm around the man's neck, he clamped down with all his remaining strength.

This is the end.

It was obvious that the man was bleeding out. Briggs kept his cheek pressed tightly against his neck in order to keep him under control. He could feel his heart beat fading, there was nothing left in this enemy now. He offered little resistance and barely tugged at Briggs's right arm in a feeble attempt to free himself from the choking grip.

Briggs felt his strength fading. Blood saturated his clothes. It was quiet now, disturbingly quiet. No noise from the street could be heard in the darkness, but a sound broke through that rattled Briggs to his soul.

"Please," the man whispered in perfect English. "Please." He gently patted Briggs's right arm. "Please let go."

Eyes wide, Briggs loosened his grip, just enough to allow the man to breathe. He rolled off the man onto his side.

My God. I have killed one of our own. A Seal, Recon, who? Briggs's head spun at what he had done.

"Who . . . are you?" Briggs asked, still on the floor.

"My name is Yusef Ahmed. I am Jordanian. Please do not kill me."

Perfect English, but not one of ours, thought Briggs as he tried to grasp the situation. A rush of relief overwhelmed Briggs, knowing his battle had indeed been with one of the enemy.

The smell of the Jordanian's open stomach assaulted Briggs's nostrils, and again he choked back vomit.

"I'm sorry I . . . shot you," the Jordanian said in a weak, broken voice. He began to mumble a prayer in Arabic as the life spilled from his body onto the floor. Briggs could feel the man's artery pulsing in his neck. *Bump, bump, bump.* The heartbeats came slower and slower, and then one last soft *bump.*

Oh God. Briggs let go and pulled himself up to a sitting position, his back leaning against the cold wall. After a few deep breaths, he probed the Jordanian's body, looking for weapons, information, anything. Moving his hands slowly around the dead man, he accidentally slid his hand into the gaping wound he had inflicted.

It was too much. Briggs lost control and vomited.

This is so fucked up. They taught me how to use a knife to kill a man in training, but they neglected to tell me the part about how long it takes for a man to bleed to death. And this sure as shit isn't the way it looks in the movies. He slumped back against the wall and moments passed like hours—numb, sitting in the dark, waiting, contemplating what to do. Above, he could hear voices muffled by the rubble and debris from the roof of the building.

Should he cry out or keep quiet? It was hard to tell who had come out on top of the firefight. The automatic fire and RPGs seemed to come from everywhere. His fire team was small that morning, only fourteen men. It could be bad topside.

Briggs shut off his mind, stayed numb, poised, and silent. Better to wait it out than risk another face–to-face with Death. He'd already had enough in this short span to last a lifetime.

"Briggs!" Soft at first, almost out of range.

Then again. "Briggs!" He recognized American voices, English. His name.

"Down here!" he yelled as loudly as he could. The effort brought incredible pain. He clenched his teeth and cried out again, "Down here!"

Then he lost consciousness.

When Briggs woke up, he was in the back of a Humvee. The first face he saw was that of Lt. Col. Check, who had a neat trickle of blood running down the left side of his face from a cut above his eye.

"How ya feel, Briggs?" Check asked, leaning over him.

"I'm not sure . . . a little weird, sir."

"That's the morphine. He slapped Briggs lightly on the thigh. "You're okay. Just a little shot up, but it's nothing that won't grow back. By the way, the corpsman checked you out. You still got your dick."

Briggs started to laugh but winced in pain, bringing his right arm across his body to gently hold his injured left arm. "Oh, don't make me laugh, sir."

Check laughed, this time slapping his own thigh. "Okay, Briggs. You're on your way to Balad Hospital, so just relax for now. You will be back in the fight in no time."

"Back home? No . . . I mean, no sir. I'm good to go, sir. Don't send me home. I'm okay, I swear." Briggs was trying to sit up as he rambled on, the morphine doing most of the talking.

"Whoa there, Devil Dog," Check said, gently pushing him back. "You're not going home. I said you were going to Balad. Do you think I would send back a badass like you? Hell no! You're going to have to get shot up a lot worse than this, big guy." He glanced over at the corpsman holding up the IV, who nodded his head in agreement.

"Lieutenant Colonel's right, Briggs. You'll be back at it in no time."

The conversation was wiggling its way through the morphine to some brief glint of understanding. Briggs looked up at Check, pointing curiously at the bleeding. "Damn, sir, you're hurt."

"Hurt? Hell no! I'm not hurt. This is just a nick from the front sight post of your platoon commander's rifle. When the firefight started, he ran so damn fast for cover he swung his weapon into my face," Check said, chuckling. "Hell, it was all I could do to keep the blood out of my eyes to see. Damndest thing is the entire squad is fine. You and I are the only ones hurt—well, you're the only one hurt—and there are eleven dead bad guys stacked up in the back of a truck. Eleven! In fact, I'd bet if I'd been standing next to your bad ass when all hell broke loose, I wouldn't have this shiner.

"Oh, by the way," Check leaned over close to Briggs's ear, "the corpsman who cut your camo bottoms off and checked you out . . . well, I think he's a little sweet on you. He might be queer for your gear." Check roared in another fit of laughter.

Briggs's face turned red as he fought his own laughter and the pain that came from the effort. "Please . . . don't . . . don't make me laugh, sir. Man, that hurts."

Check smiled. He then produced the Ka-Bar. "Here. The guy you left this with is finished with it." He slid the twelve-inch knife back into the scabbard on Briggs's cartridge belt that was on the deck beside him and clipped the safety strap. "That's an old-school Ka-Bar from Vietnam. Where did you come by it?"

"It was my father's. It really came in handy."

"Yes it did, my friend. When this is all over, we'll smoke one of my good cigars and share some killer scotch—pardon the pun." Check winked and held his index finger to his lips. Briggs returned the wink and gave in to the euphoria of the morphine.

CHAPTER SIX

June 2005

His first encounter with the dark side of the memories of his first kill was at Balad Military Hospital, just outside of Bagdad, the same day as the firefight. Briggs woke near midnight. Gone now was the fog of painkillers. He was aware of where he was. His bandaged wounds were a visible reminder. With an urgent need to empty his bladder, he swung his legs off the bed, barely feeling any pain. With no IV in his arm now, he moved freely around the room. There were four beds, but he was the only occupant.

It was extremely quiet in this area of the field hospital. The hatch leading to his room was open, and across the hallway, he noticed a bathroom sign on the bulkhead with an arrow pointing to the head. He stepped into the dimly lit passageway and found it. As he went to open the door, he looked down at the bandage on his right hand. He wasn't quite sure how he'd injured his hand or how much damage had been done. It hurt—no doubt about that—but he could flex it and move all of his fingers. He squinted, trying to remember more, then shrugged, opened the door, and flipped on the light. Carefully, he unwrapped the long strip of gauze, knowing he would have to wrap it back so as not to piss off the corpsman. His eyes strained to focus on the red, puffy burn on the palm of his hand. Briggs moved back into the passageway and stood under the overhead light. The burn held the telling shape of an AK-47 flash suppressor, seared into his hand where he'd grabbed the hot barrel of the Jordanian's rifle.

Suddenly, the flashback to the horrific struggle for his life drove him to his knees. Freefalling in time, he was back in that dark basement. Terror grabbed his soul, forcing him to relive the entire event right there in the passageway. He could smell his own vomit intermingled with the smell of the man's entrails. It was too much. He wept.

Bang!

He was certain he'd just heard an enormous explosion.

Not again. He whimpered and shook his head to break the memory of the dying man's cries.

In an attempt to escape the flashback, he stood up and ran, turning to his left, and then quickly to his right. He was disorientated. In his confusion, he bounced off the bulkhead, and then another and another. He had no idea where he was. One passageway and bulkhead after another, he crashed, bouncing left and right until he found himself outside the building. He couldn't tell which was darker, the place in his head or the moonless desert. Briggs ran to a short fence a few yards away, his stomach churning, and finally retched until everything inside of him poured onto the sand and splashed onto his bare feet.

"Briggs?"

The voice was familiar but faint, barely piercing the fog of his delirium. He froze.

Check put his hand on Briggs's shoulder.

"No!" Briggs hollered as he turned and grabbed Check's arm. Check countered the swing and spun Briggs on his heels, gently sliding him to the ground in a squat, holding him from behind.

"Aaah! My God, nooo!" Briggs howled.

"It's okay. Let it go, son. You're safe. You're safe," Check said in a low voice near Briggs's ear, rocking him slightly. "You're not there. You're here. You're safe. Open your eyes, son. Look up at the stars. Smell the fresh air. You're here, not there."

The mantra slowly found its way in, until Briggs came back to the reality of his surroundings: the familiar voice of a comrade, the healing powers of fresh air. He opened his eyes to see the brilliant heavens. His panic started to ease, his breathing calmed.

Check had rescued him once again from the dark, but this time he was fighting a memory that no weapon could defeat.

Briggs looked over at Check with surprise. "What are you doing here, sir?"

"I came to check on you and do a little paperwork. You look good. Out for a little stroll?" He grinned at Briggs.

"Not sure."

"Come on now, let me take you back to your rack," Check said as he started to pull Briggs up by his shoulders.

Briggs protested. "No, let me stay out here. I need the air. I've . . . I've got to stay out here." Refusing Check's help, he scooted across the ground a short distance to lean against the wall of the building, looking out into the pitch-dark desert.

Check settled in next to him, staring into the dark. Briggs felt much calmer now, thankfully far away from that place of terror—if not in spirit, at least for the moment in physical form.

"Thank you, sir." He raised his chin and looked up at the stars, allowing the tears to flow down his cheek.

Check squinted his eyes and said in a gentle voice, "You know, Briggs . . . hell, I know you know, but I gotta say it."

Briggs waited patiently, watching Check out of the corner of his eye as he struggled to form his words.

"You're not the first person to go through this, and you need to hear this from someone who knows it's okay to cry, because it is, damn it. I've been in that same dark hell you're in right now. You gotta remember how you got out of the darkness, because it's going to happen again. Be ready for it. And each time, you need to leave a trail of breadcrumbs so you can find your way back, and each time you make your way back you will be stronger: physically, mentally, spiritually. I will not tell you that one day all the bad thoughts will go away, just that it gets easier after a while. The memories don't burn as bad after you've fought your way back a few times through the torture of your own recollections." He paused and turned to look at Briggs. His eyes were filled with the intensity of a warrior.

"All's I'm saying, Briggs, is that if you let it control you, it will not only destroy your career, but your life. So just fucking fight it, is what I'm tellin' ya. Fight it now and fight it as hard as you can. Don't let it take you. Ever."

Briggs stared at him for a long time, silent. Then he looked at the night sky.

Check sighed. "There, I just saved you at least two years of psychobabble bullshit. That's about how long it took my psychologist to give me those few words of wisdom, and it didn't cost you a hundred hours of your life at two hundred fifty bucks an hour."

Check shifted his position and stared out into the night sky as he continued. "I remember with crystal clarity the exact moment my life was forever changed. October 23, 1983, a beautiful Sunday morning at 0622. My life is still often frozen in that hellish moment. Sundays were supposed to be calm and quiet, you know? Get a little extra rack time and then play some b-ball in the parking lot after a late breakfast."

He was quiet for some time before he spoke again. He spoke clearly and quietly, confessing his unbearable mistake in gruesome detail to the ears of the night and a young man who desperately needed to hear them. Briggs sensed the gravity and importance of the conversation. This was not a war story, nor was it a man bragging. It was therapeutic. Something he knew he should pay close attention to because he would have to learn how to share his story in order to survive his own nightmare.

"I was in Lebanon, the 24th Marine Amphibious Unit and its Battalion Landing Team 1/8, when the barracks were bombed and so many great men, my friends, were killed."

Check's eyes glazed over as he continued talking. "I was in charge of a small recon squad on its way back from checking out the hillsides around the airport. Hezbollah and their snipers were using the positions above the Marine barracks to take pop shots at us and occasionally lob a mortar or two in our direction."

Briggs sat quietly as Check talked.

"They were extremely tough to catch. They would squeeze off a couple of rifle rounds, or use a small mortar, then hide their weapons and fade away into the countryside or the town. We knew that if a reconnaissance squad could stay above the enemy in the hills and be quiet long enough without being noticed by one of the locals, the squad could envelop them."

Check's jaw clenched. "The squad was returning from patrol, weaving its way between houses and stone walls on the way down the hill when we noticed a large yellow Mercedes truck meandering along. One of my men tapped me on the shoulder and said, 'This doesn't look right, sir.' We stopped and watched the driver for a few seconds."

Briggs knew from recent experience that those few seconds would tick away in Check's head for the rest of his days.

"The rules of engagement were simple. We could not even put a round in the chamber unless we were being shot at. Here was a man who'd met all the criteria of a bad guy. He had a long, black beard, was in a large truck all by himself, and was driving with no apparent sense of direction on a day that was not a usual delivery day. Normally the drivers who came to the base to deliver supplies had at least two guys in the truck."

Check's eyes were black holes of pain as he looked at Briggs. "The only thing I did right was to close in on the guy from the hillside to get a better look. Whether we spooked the driver or just arrived at the exact moment the driver decided to attack, I'll never know. No matter. The man drove two big loops around the parking lot in front of the barracks, then slammed on the gas, heading straight for the gate."

Check told Briggs that he went with the rules of engagement instead of instinct. The politics of warfare kept running through his head. The man wasn't shooting at him and had no weapon, so he should do nothing. But the Marine in him wanted to shoot the bastard and shoot like hell! His mind raced through several scenarios at once. Should he give the order to fire on the truck and stop it? What if he was wrong? What if it was just a truck delivering supplies? If he started shooting without cause, they were all screwed.

Check's voice was low as he continued. "Scanning the ranks of my men now running to my side with their weapons at the ready, I heard the sobering sound of brass slamming into the chamber of M-16s and M-60s. I quickly returned my attention to the speeding truck, now only a hundred yards from the gate to the Marine barracks compound. It was hard to tell with all the dust if the truck was slowing for the sentry.

"Instinctively, I knew the Mercedes was not going to slow down. I knew it in my gut. Still, I argued with myself, not wanting to be trigger-happy, not wanting to make everything worse, if that was even possible. I kept watching, thinking, 'He's going to stop, he's going to stop.'

"He didn't stop. And I had waited too long."

Check went quiet.

Briggs found himself trying to catch his breath. He had no idea what to say. He forced himself to take in a breath, to blink his eyes and relax his hands, which seemed to be clenched to the point of pain. He was waiting for the story to come to a climax, to come to an end. Every Marine knew the story of the barracks bombing, but only the Marines who were there knew the true horror of it. And with each word from Check, Briggs was being pulled into the reality of that horrible day in Marine history.

"Those frail second thoughts shattered before my eyes. I was helpless to change the course of events as they would unfold. The confirmation of my worst expectations came from behind me. My platoon sergeant spoke out in a loud, clear voice. 'Damn, Lieutenant, that truck is going to ram the gate!' I flung my M-16 onto my shoulder and cleared the safety, as did all the Marines in the vicinity. *Follow the leader.* I lowered my weapon and called out to my men to do the same. I realized that the main-gate guards and the barracks were in the line of fire and would most likely be hit by the devastating amount of firepower my men would lay down in order to stop the truck. Instead, the men in the sentry towers would have to be responsible for stopping the truck with their M-60s.

"Despite every indication to the contrary, I found myself thinking again, 'What if we're wrong?'

"Then someone shouted, 'Sir, are we going to shoot or what? Sir!'

"It was too late. The truck crashed through the gate and into the courtyard of the main barracks. The vehicle made a nosedive into the main lobby next to the entranceway and stopped. For just an instant, there was nothing—no sound, no movement, and no explosion. Everything was suspended in a giant held breath of *what the fuck*? And then time shifted once again."

Check shifted from side to side, the sand and gravel grinding beneath his boots and hips. He was digging into the dirt, as if he were preparing to share the true horror of his memories and preparing himself for the onslaught of emotions that piggybacked themselves to the experience. Briggs knew Check was about to unleash the real truth of his pain. They both paused to take in one last breath before Check shed light on his true demon.

"I could see the bright-white flash of the explosion as it radiated from the center of the Mercedes truck and fanned out in an incredible spectrum of red, yellow, orange, and black. So much black. Everything slowed or seemed to just not move at all. I felt like I was watching it happen an instant at a time, as if someone were clicking a remote. *Stop. Play. Stop. Play.* There was no time, there was no sound. I was transfixed on every slight movement. I could not move. The entire building lifted off the ground and seemed to hover in the air for a fraction of time. Smoke bellowed out of its belly as it rose from its foundation.

"Still, I did not move. I just stood there, a little under two hundred yards away, watching, mesmerized by the blast, knowing that in an instant it would be in my face, burning and pelting my body with flying debris and shrapnel. A fitting reward.

"I just stood there, cursed, feeling the massive weight of the deaths of my fellow Marines bearing down on my soul."

"Damn," Briggs said.

"Damn is just about right," Check said, his face skyward, a catch in his voice. He paused for a long time before he continued. "My platoon sergeant tackled me from behind, knocking me to the ground. He covered me with his own body. Against my own will to survive, I did, by the hand of another."

Check groaned as he pulled himself to his feet. Briggs did the same and leaned against the bulkhead.

"Those of us in the front of the formation were covered with dust, dirt, and fist-sized pieces of rock and brick. I jumped to my feet and ran to the barracks. I didn't even turn to see if my own men were okay. I couldn't bear the thought of what I might see. I just ran as fast as I could. When I reached the fireball that was once the truck, the roar of fire wasn't as deafening and the dust had settled just enough for me to make out the building. I looked up and saw several bodies sandwiched between collapsed concrete floors. Some were still moving. I had to act, to do something, to save the wounded, to try to make up for what I had caused."

Briggs started to say something, but Check held up his hand.

"Oh, there's more, son," he said. "I took a step to my left and bumped into something. When I looked down, I saw the torso of a Marine, cut in half just above the waist, lying face up with his eyes and mouth wide open, having seen a different level to the horror that I had shamefully witnessed, that I had caused. The blood oozed bright red and his skin was pink, and I found myself frozen again, overcome with the reality of what had happened and the overwhelming task before me of digging out the bodies of all my friends. I watched as the mouth of the Marine at my feet slowly closed and his eyes rolled back. The next instant, a small secondary explosion went off, no more than fifty feet to my left."

Check reached over to rub his left arm, which was scarred and burned and void of hair. The rippled, discolored tissue rose from his arm like wrinkled pink paper. The only place on his arm below the elbow that was not burned was the patch of skin that had been under the watch he'd worn that day.

"When I came to, I was onboard a ship. Most of the explosion hit my flak jacket and upper thighs. If I hadn't been looking down at the dead Marine at my feet, I would have gotten a face peel that would have made me look like ground hamburger, and I would definitely be blind.

"The last image in my head, boy, was the dead Marine's face and the thought that it was my fault, that I could have prevented it. This guilt was compounded by the fact that I wasn't able to help rescue those who were suffering under the collapsed walls of the barracks."

"Damn," said Briggs again.

Check nodded and pursed his lips. "Hmm, maybe *damned* is more like it. I was sent home to heal for thirty days and then to base operations stateside for over a year, stuck behind a desk with that explosion going off in my head every three minutes. When I closed my eyes, that Marine's face would reappear. I knew I needed help. I couldn't stay awake at work because I couldn't sleep at home. The nights were the worst. Insomnia doesn't even cover it. It's an exhausting abyss, boy. I wore out my mattress tossing and turning, flipping and flopping, with no light, no rest." He wiped away the tears from his eyes.

Briggs nodded, silent, somber. *My time is coming for much of the same.*

Check continued, "I am not one for drugs, so sleeping pills were out of the question, and drinking just turned me into a crying drunk, so I started seeing a psychologist." His eyes glistened with tears.

"They sent me home to hell, not to heal. My girlfriend of two years left me, and I lost any chance at a command and questioned every decision I ever made. The next thing I would lose would be my mind—this I knew. The one thing I am certain of is that if I'd been conscious after the explosion and heard the screams of the men trapped and dying in that barracks—well, that would more than likely have pushed me over the edge."

Check paused and turned to Briggs. "So fight it, Briggs, and if you can't do it alone, get help. But not through the Corps—that'd be a career killer. It is a secret you have to share with someone you trust, or it will consume you. Do you have anyone you trust, Briggs?"

Briggs shrugged, sniffed. He looked up at the starlit sky. The question hung there, unanswered. "This is a pitiful conversation, two grown men hashing over their tragedies."

"I'm afraid you're wrong there, my friend. When we get a chance, and under better circumstances, I will break out some of my good scotch. I have a few bottles of sixteen-year-old Lagavulin stashed away; I'm saving it for better times." Check chuckled low, a half smile on his lips. "You know, the one good thing that came out of that god-awful experience was getting a taste for fine scotch whiskey." Check placed a hand on Briggs's shoulder and lifted his face to the stars. "Thank God for the Scots."

"You said I was wrong," Briggs said. "What was I wrong about?"

"Don't you know?"

"Not sure, really."

Check threw his arm around Briggs's shoulders as they walked back toward the door to the hospital. "We're not hashing out our tragedies, my friend. We are healing wounds."

CHAPTER SEVEN

October 2005

After his first combat, subsequent injury, and first kill, Briggs spent twenty-one days in the hospital for his recovery. He was promoted to corporal while he was there. The promotion ceremony was quick and sterile, just like the hospital. The lingering aroma of rubbing alcohol and cleaning fluids added to his depression. Not one of his friends was there to shake his hand and congratulate him, but that was a good thing as well. It meant that no one else was hurt. He gladly would've traded the extra stripe to be back with his platoon in combat.

The physical therapy was the toughest part, but that went by rapidly as Briggs recovered from his wounds. After just a few months, he was able to fly home for his allotted ten days, basking in the sun, hoping he would not run into Anita—and at the same time, hoping he would.

His return to Iraq in October 2005 brought a sense of solidarity and fulfillment. The guilt he had felt about leaving his platoon to fight without him diminished the second his boots hit the ground. He rejoined his battalion and platoon with a renewed sense of purpose. He settled into the new accommodations and immediately performed a headcount of everyone there, relieved to see all his friends present and accounted for.

His new digs were a twelve-by-twenty rat hole in an old hotel that his platoon commander—while setting up their regimental office—had appropriated for their purposes. The building was one of several that had been abandoned during the war in Baghdad. It was over three stories tall with a single window per room—no closet, no AC, no carpet, but lots of dust, which constantly blew in, out, and up every time anything moved. There were no screens on the windows to prevent the invasion of flies, nor did most of the windows close, and if they did, it wasn't enough to keep out the stench from beyond the building's outer walls. Depending on each Marine's time spent in the armpit of Baghdad, the odors were either barely tolerable or par for the course.

For Briggs, there was one particularly foul smell that never left him, not even when he was sitting on a dock six thousand miles away on the Outer Banks of North Carolina. It was the smell of burning flesh and hair, intermingled with sulfur and magnesium. It clung to the back of his throat like bile he could not wash away. It permeated his nose, played with his reality, reminded him of the sounds of screaming—his own as well as others. Screams of war.

After his company commander had claimed the abandoned building for his men, a skinny Iraqi man wearing dirty, baggy pants and an equally disgusting collarless shirt showed up, claiming to own the building, and demanding that he be paid rent. The commander—reluctantly, but for the sake of peace—agreed to pay the paltry sum.

In November, a month after arriving back in country, Briggs met his new staff NCO, Staff Sergeant Martin.

"What are you reading?" Martin asked, peering over Briggs's shoulder as he lay stretched out on his rack.

"David Baldacci," Briggs said, holding the book, *Last Man Standing*, in the air above his head. "There was a stack of care-package stuff in the mess hall. I found this at the bottom. Good thing, because it's really good. I got lucky, I think." Briggs smiled.

"Nice. Hey, how's the arm and everything?"

"Good as ever. See?" Briggs held up his left arm, wiggled his fingers and thumb, then popped himself in the chest with his right arm. "I can still pull a trigger *and* pick my nose," he joked.

"Good thing—you'll probably have to do both tomorrow. We're going out on roadside checks. Be ready." Without another word, Martin turned and left the room.

◆

The next day, Briggs was up long before he needed to be; he just couldn't sleep. His detachment of six Marines would be taking new Iraqi policemen out on their first day of work, four miles outside the Green Zone. It was always hectic and confusing the first time out, especially with language difficulties and dealing with the flow of traffic. Nerves would be spring-loaded all damn day. All it took was an odd look from a local to tighten up your ass enough to split quarters. A good night's rest was mandatory for the day ahead, but rest just didn't seem to be in the cards for Briggs.

They loaded into Humvees with heavy up armor just before sunrise to beat the traffic that would soon back up the streets in wheeled chaos. Three miles into the city, along a narrow two-lane street, an IED exploded off to the side of Briggs's truck, causing the driver to steer the vehicle hard left onto the elevated sidewalk in front of a three-story building. The gun battle that followed scattered the remaining vehicles, as the Marines entered the buildings and streets, fighting from the cover of doorways and flipped civilian vehicles.

Air support arrived quickly but strained to differentiate the enemy, dressed in civilian garb, firing from their positions in the crowd. They were also inhibited by the fleeing civilians trying to avoid the overwhelming barrage of RPGs and small arms fire that seemed to come from every direction. The indiscriminant fire had no prejudice between uniforms or children—it rained down on all.

Briggs struggled to extricate himself from the front seat of the Humvee. As he swung the door open, the butt of his rifle sling got caught on the center console of the vehicle. He leaned back in to untangle the sling when several rounds bounced off the inside of the door. The sling popped loose and he fell to the ground, quickly picking himself up and running for cover.

That was lucky, he thought as he ran around the front of the truck in the direction of the building where other Marines had already found good cover.

Small arms fire riddled the side of the truck and the street. Two RPGs landed underneath the front of the Humvee and exploded, lifting it two feet into the air, then bouncing it back on its tires.

Briggs skidded into the building on his knees and fell in place next to Lance Corporal Jeff Blake, who was quickly setting up protective fire.

Briggs had met Blake two days ago. Blake had a fair amount of combat experience and had been nominated for the Silver Star for bravery, something few Marines received.

"Good company here," Briggs said as he took up position near Blake in the blown-out window next to the door.

"What's that you say?" Blake asked. Briggs steadied his weapon and fired at insurgents across the street.

"Nothing!" Briggs shouted. "Are you okay?"

"Peachy, just peachy," Blake replied. He fired several shots at the upper floors of the building across the street. Without glancing away from the sights of his rifle, he added, "Nice day for a gunfight, don't you think?"

Brevity in combat was an excellent cloak for those who were composed and scared as hell at the same time.

Briggs smiled and shook his head as he kept his eyes on his rifle sights.

The Marines had all made it to cover and were returning fire, but it seemed as if every window on the top floor of every building had a rifle barrel sticking out of it, blazing away.

Blake fired off a full clip of thirty and turned to start up the stairs of the building without saying a word.

Briggs turned to him. "What are you doing?"

"The war's upstairs, man," Blake replied and bolted for the flight of steps. Briggs got up and started behind him. On the way, he grabbed the arm of one of his fire team leaders who had taken cover with them.

"Cover that door, then follow," Briggs ordered. The Marine nodded and Briggs ran for the steps to catch up with Blake. As he hit the first step, an explosion sounded behind him. The head and right shoulder of the fire team leader flew across the room and landed near his feet. There was nothing to do for the Marine. His body was fractured into pieces, splattered all over the room and ceiling. Briggs clenched his teeth, emotion welling up, which he forced back down. He resumed his ascent behind Blake.

On the second floor, he found Blake standing at a large fractured hole in the wall, facing the street. An incoming round missed Blake and struck the doorjamb by Briggs's cheek, showering him with wood splinters. He dove to the deck as a second round splintered the concrete near Blake, sending fragments into Briggs's eyes. He quickly rolled over, blinking furiously. Blake backed away from the window to the far wall after he had dispatched the shooter directly across the street.

"You okay?" Blake asked.

Briggs didn't respond.

"Well, ya better get up. Bastards are pretty pissed. We'll be getting incoming any second!" With that, Blake grabbed Briggs with one arm, jerking him to his feet.

Blake was six feet three and nothing but pure power. A fullback at Texas A&M, he was destined for the pros, but he gave it all up in his junior year and joined the Marines as an enlisted man.

Briggs still didn't respond but moved like a puppet under Blake's commands. He was still trying to regain his mental footing. He just missed being shot, one of his fellow Marines just blew up in front of him, he was being tossed around like a rag doll by a mammoth of a man who had no regard for his own safety, and now he was pinned to the deck by incoming small arms fire.

"Come on, man! You're going to get killed if you stay here."

They cleared the room just as automatic fire entered the window and mortar holes, bouncing around the entire room. At the top of the next flight of stairs, they ran head-on into two teenage boys with AK-47s. A quick burst from Blake's weapon and both fell dead on the floor. Blake continued his charge down the hallway, checking each room along the way. Briggs provided cover.

While running backward to cover Blake's advance, Briggs noticed a rope tied to a post and dangling from the window on the backside of the building. It was the way out for the two boys Blake had just shot.

"Hold up, Blake!" Briggs shouted as he looked out the window and saw two more ropes hanging from one floor up. "I think we got at least two more up above us."

"I got 'em," Blake said without hesitation as he bolted for the ladder well.

"No! Wait!" Briggs called. They needed a plan, but Blake was on his way up and could not be stopped.

"Shit," Briggs spat as he ran back to the window. If he waited, he could shoot whomever started down the ropes. Still, Briggs knew Blake would need cover, and there was no time to think about what needed to be done or to yell out to him. Even though the firefight was raging with noise and explosions, he didn't want to give away Blake's assault on the floor above him. So he quietly waited, and prepared, and just as he predicted, it happened.

Briggs could hear Blake begin firing his M4 with no return fire. For the moment, Blake appeared to have the upper hand. Suddenly, Briggs noticed one of the escape ropes had a leg attached to it, swinging out of the third-floor window.

Wait, Briggs thought. *Wait for it.* Then another body started down the same rope. *Just a little more.* Then the second rope swayed as a man swung his leg around it. Gunshots followed. A man who was apparently lined up to follow the first man on this second rope fell headfirst through the window, knocking the first man off the rope. At that point, Briggs opened fire on the two shimmying down the first rope, nearest to him. Just two shots and Briggs watched both boys fall to the ground and lie motionless, crumpled on top of one another. Above, Blake stuck his head out of the window and shot the man who had been knocked off the rope as he was reaching for his weapon. Blake motioned for Briggs to join him on the third floor.

Briggs bolted up the stairs to the third floor where Blake was standing at an open window, firing on the building across the street. The sight unnerved Briggs—and pissed him off.

"Why the hell are you so reckless with your life, man?" Briggs asked as he pulled Blake down, out of the line of fire.

"Maybe I don't have a life worth a crap, and maybe it's not worth trying to protect," Blake belted out. He struggled free of Briggs and ran to the other side of the room, passing two windows. As he did, he drew fire from the street below and the adjacent building, glass flying in all directions and chips of brick showering over his head. He then quickly splayed across the floor and slid into the next room, crawling to the ladder well. Briggs quickly followed. The sound of the bullets bouncing and skipping off the walls and floor were deafening. This seemed to be no concern to Blake as he stood up, positioned himself next to open windows and mortar holes, and took deadly aim to hold 'em and squeeze 'em with little regard for proper protective cover that would limit his exposure to incoming fire. His Wild West show was a hit or kill for every round he fired.

"There's another one who won't be shooting back!" he yelled as he turned from the window and headed down another set of stairs.

"Where in the hell are we going?" Briggs shouted as he ran wide around the open wall and window in an effort to keep up.

"I know a way out of here. Stay close."

"And keep my head down, right?" Briggs replied as he struggled to run across the broken concrete and rubble strewn about the floor.

"That's up to you, dude. It's your ass," said Blake, now in a full run for the next ladder well. He rounded a corner at the bottom of the broken ladder well, where several fractured slabs of concrete lay.

"Help me," Blake said. Briggs helped him move a large section of concrete from the wall, which exposed a hole leading to the basement of the building.

They jumped down into the foundation of the building, which led to a sewage system under the main street. The stench was unbearable and Briggs's stomach lurched as he held back the urge to vomit. Once inside the six-foot sewer pipe, they slowed to a walk and headed in the direction of the flow of the ankle-deep ooze of sewage.

"Man, this sucks. It would be nice if these people were savvier about good sanitation."

"Yeah, I know what you mean. They just kind of let it all roll into the river."

"Right. Where are we going, Blake?"

"To the other side of the street and up through the basement of the other building. It's target rich, dude! Besides, we've already killed all the bad guys in this structure."

Briggs held up his hands. "No, man, that's not the plan. We need to come out down the street at the end of this row of buildings so we can help cover the guys pinned down."

Blake sloshed onward. "Can't do that. This pipe runs in a straight line to the river, just a little over six hundred yards. But I think it connects to the next building."

"No, we head for the river and come back up at the end of the street. If we come up in that building, we'll get our asses shot off by the bad guys *and* our guys. We should—"

"Are you kidding, dude?" Blake interrupted. "We kicked ass together. Let's go for it!"

"No!" Briggs barked. "This is my show, and I am in charge, got it?"

"Yeah, I got it. We do it your way, Corporal," Blake replied as he led on through the dark pipe, the only hint of light coming from the opening they'd made behind them and the exit at the river six hundred yards in front of them.

With heavy breaths, Blake said, "Okay, at the end of this main pipe, we'll come to an opening just outside the edge of the river. That's where it can get a little dicey."

"Dicey?"

"You never know who's at the other end," Blake said. "If it's the bad guys, they are probably sleeping or fucking off, so we stand a good chance of getting clear. If it's good guys, you can bet your ass they're newbies put out on security watch and they are freaked out and trigger-happy. Announce ourselves to the wrong guys and we're dead. Announce ourselves to the right guys with no password and they start shooting into the drainpipe before we clear the opening. It's a shit-luck deal. I personally would rather sneak up on the bad guys at the next basement and shoot their asses."

"How do you know all this shit?" Briggs asked.

"You don't do three tours in this shithole without learning a few tricks, Corporal. Besides, I've been in firefights on this street before. We found a group of bad guys using this pipe for their snipers. We couldn't figure out how many snipers were shooting at us until we found this pipe connecting the two buildings and then on to the river. So we blew shut the two openings under the buildings. It figures that they would reopen them, or at least that's what I was betting on." Blake bent over just enough to clear the top of the pipe.

They stopped at the break in the pipe that led to the basement of the building across the street. It was covered with heavy rock and dirt.

"Too bad. Looks like we'll have to take the long way around after all," Blake said as he squinted to see down the pipe. They walked in silence. At the end of the drain they found the opening.

After exiting the pipe, Blake turned around and stood there. He stared at a set of footprints frozen in the mud, frozen in time, frozen in the maddening heat of this place.

"What are you looking at?" Briggs asked.

"I'm taking a piss. I would hate to get into another gunfight and piss my pants because I didn't take the time when I had a chance. I don't think the bad guys would stop shooting at me if I asked for a piss break. Do you?"

Briggs shook his head and moved toward the higher ground without responding.

CHAPTER EIGHT

October 2005

Blake had lied about having to relieve himself. It was just an excuse so he could collect his thoughts. The tracks on the ground brought back a powerful ghost, one that haunted him relentlessly. The footprints led into and out of the six-foot sewer pipe. The prints were deep and long—the tracks of a big man carrying a heavy burden in and out. They were his own tracks from almost a year ago, still waiting for the rainy season to mercifully release them from the mud that had turned them into concrete, baked by the blazing summer sun. Not even the edges had broken down and tumbled inward. They were sharp and jagged, like tall prison walls, holding in the memories of the day Blake had been here— the day he had carried his friend's limp body into the pipe after drawing machine-gun fire from across the river. Blake had run with his friend slung over his shoulder, hoping he would be okay. "Stay cool, bro. I got you." Blake had said, out of breath.

PFC Kyle Dunn was from Iowa. He was tall and skinny, countless freckles dotting his face and arms. His fair Irish skin turned as red as his hair almost immediately the day he stepped off the transport plane at Al Asad Air Base. The firefight started at the top of the hill above the sewer pipe. When Dunn had taken cover along with the rest of his fire team by the riverbank, someone started shooting from across the river, more than six hundred yards away. Spotting the pipe, Dunn and the others had quickly run for it—knowing it might be booby-trapped or the enemy might already be inside. It was better than getting cut to pieces on the open banks of the Tigris River. PFC Dunn had slipped and slid almost the entire way down the reed-covered bank into the water. A steady rain fell—just enough to turn the gray and tan soil into a flowing slur as slippery as grease.

Several rounds had whizzed past Blake's head and splashed with a muddy thump in front of him. Then another thump shook him to his core—the sound of a round impacting flesh followed by a scream of pain. Ahead of him, Dunn collapsed, blood pouring from his right thigh. Blake quickly jerked Dunn to his feet. He knew Kyle would not make it back up the hill on his own.

"Hold on!" Blake had shouted as he lifted Kyle effortlessly up and onto his shoulder. He turned to run up the bank, getting good traction as he dug into the slippery ground. His fire team had made it into the pipe and started returning fire in order to cover Blake's ascent up the bank. He ran with long, powerful strides, like a football player crossing over the field with the goalpost in sight.

Thump! Thump, thump! Several rounds splashed at his feet and on the bank in front of him. And then once more . . . *thump.* In a split second, Blake felt Dunn's weapon fall to the ground, then saw it sink into the three-inch mud, the bloody sling floating on top of the sludge. Then Blake felt an intense pain in his left armpit. "Damn it!" he'd screamed. The pain was so intense, his knees started to buckle and his stomach wrenched in response. One of the bullets had passed through Dunn's body into Blake's. He kept moving, reaching the safety of the pipe, and placed Dunn's limp body on the ground.

He quickly rolled Dunn over onto his stomach in order to assess his wounds. Blood flowed from Dunn's leg and from under the bottom edge of his flak jacket. He didn't move, not even a twitch. The corpsman took over immediately, and Blake returned to join the men still firing across the river.

The incoming fire had stopped and the sergeant in charge was waving his hands and shouting, "Cease fire, cease fire!"

Everyone obeyed . . . except Blake.

He stood without cover and fired wildly, fully exposed, walking toward the banks of the Tigris River, emptying magazines and quickly reloading as he walked, screaming at the top of his lungs. A trail of empty magazines lay behind him every third or fourth step until he reached Kyle's weapon submerged in the mud. The fatal hit.

The eight Marines in the fire team stood quietly as they witnessed a hero entangled in anguish for a fallen brother. Blake stopped and screamed out one last time, spreading his arms wide, his smoking weapon in his left hand and his clenched right fist shaking in defiance. Raindrops turned into white vapor as they struck the hot barrel of his weapon.

"I'm still here, you bastards!"

That was the last drop of rain that fell on the bloody ground for almost a year.

Blake had leaned down and picked up his friend's weapon. In his last act of defiance, he turned his back on the riverbank and picked up his discarded magazines as he returned to his team.

"You okay?" his sergeant had asked, knowing what the answer would be from the big man but asking anyway.

"Yeah, I'm cool."

He wasn't though, and the corpsman knew it because he'd seen the exit wound on PFC Dunn's body and knew from the way Blake was carrying himself that it had hit Blake as well—somewhere. There was so much blood on Blake, it was hard to tell. They waited for a helicopter to take away Dunn's body. When it arrived, the corpsman told Blake to get on it too.

"No" was his reply.

The corpsman asked to see his wound.

"It's okay, Doc. I'm good."

"Then show me," he insisted. "Look, if it's just a scratch, you can walk home with us. Come on, you haven't even looked yourself. You are probably in shock."

"I'm not!"

"That's not your call. It's mine. Now if you don't show me, I'm going to tell the sergeant, and he will make you fly out," the corpsman said with authority.

"Fine."

Blake removed his body armor and then his shirt, revealing the wounds just beneath his armpit.

"Fuck!" The corpsman said as he pulled out an 8 × 8 field dressing and pressed it hard against the shredded flesh and exposed ribs under Blake's armpit. "You're on that helicopter, no more lip."

A year later, Blake reached under his armpit and placed his hand on the wound, which had required eight staples to close. He had returned to duty the next day and never complained of the injury.

"I'm still here, still here," Blake mumbled to himself.

———————

When they arrived at the area where the fighting had taken place, they found the battle had faded to a few small arms firefights in the far-off distance. Their platoon commander had arrived to assess the damage and evacuate the wounded.

"Corporal Briggs, are you and Lance Corporal Blake all right?" their lieutenant asked, briefly lifting his head from the radio to look at the two Marines.

"We're good, sir," said Briggs.

"Are you two responsible for the carnage in that building?" the lieutenant asked as he held his hand over the mic of the radio. Briggs and Blake nodded. "Highly impressive, outstanding job. The two of you have left quite a meal for the wild dogs of Baghdad to feast upon tonight. You can tell me all about it later, but for now, grab a SAW, get up on the roof of this building, and give us cover while we mop this up. Don't shoot the two guys on the other roof. I sent two men and an Iraqi up there. They have a radio, so I'll alert them that you're going up."

"Aye, sir," Briggs replied as he gathered up an additional automatic assault weapon and extra ammo from the truck and headed up the ladder with Blake following close behind. Once on the roof, Briggs took up a position overlooking the street.

"Where do you want me?" Blake asked, also carrying extra ammo.

"*You* get your ass away from me, you nutcase. I don't know what's up your ass, but you're going to get me—and anyone around you—killed. If you want to die, do everyone a favor and jump off a building higher than this one." Briggs stopped short and tried to calm himself. He was angry and getting loud. He needed to stay in control.

Briggs tried again. "What is it with you? Why in the hell do you take such chances? Are you after another Silver Star or something? Or maybe you're trying for the big one, the Medal of Honor? Well, you're not going to get it here. First chance I get, your ass is going to be someone else's problem. You are out of my platoon as soon as we get back to the Zone."

He paused, his breathing heavy. He could feel the redness in his face, his heart pounding from the sheer frustration of a Marine so wayward and reckless in the face of all this hell. "Well, what is it?" he said a little louder than he wanted to. "What is it with you, man?" He looked away. "No, you know what? I don't want to know. Just stay away from me."

Blake laughed wickedly. "Hey, I know all about you, Briggs. They call you Ripper, and that's one hell of a rep. You didn't get that nickname by playing it safe and hiding behind walls. I heard you killed three dudes with a Ka-Bar when you ran out of ammo. Carved 'em up like sushi."

Briggs had been squatting near the two-and-a-half-foot block wall that encompassed the top of the building, but he jumped to his feet behind the safety of the wall and shoved the Marine. Blake staggered backward and, off balance, dropped the ammo can he was carrying. Briggs snarled, "Shut your mouth, asshole. You don't know a damn thing about me."

"Don't try me, Briggs," Blake snapped.

"Or you'll do what? Kick my ass? I think *you* need your ass kicked. I don't trust you, Blake, and that means I don't want you around me or my men, because you're *going to die*." Briggs carefully emphasized each word. "That means when you go down dead or wounded, a good man or two will have to get your sorry ass out of whatever mess you created. That's not going to happen, not while I'm in charge. Drag your ass over to the wall facing the street, set up, and stay put." He was spitting the words now, anger boiling over.

Just as Briggs finished chewing Blake's ass, two more men came up the stairs to set up on the roof. Briggs sent them over to the far side to watch the back wall and informed them of the rope escape tactic the enemy was using. He returned to Blake, who was staring over the edge of the wall.

Briggs bit his lip, calmer now, and kicked himself for letting his temper get the best of him. He wanted to talk to Blake about his behavior, see if there was anything he could do. Blake could be a valuable asset to his platoon; however, his cavalier and reckless actions had to be stymied. Briggs sat down next to Blake with his back to the wall.

"Blake, I need to start over," he said in a softer tone. "We need to talk, not engage each other." As Briggs started to speak, this time slower and with compassion in a genuine effort to counsel him, he noticed that Blake's eyes were brimming with tears.

Whether it was something he said, the way he said it, or Blake's need to finally get the demons out of his head, Briggs didn't know, but Blake started to talk, calmly and with profound sadness, tormented with the kind of pain that could tear down the biggest and strongest of men. The anguish embedded in the fibers of his being could not be exorcised away. With the sounds of war around them, he let loose the weight of his soul to Briggs.

"You know, Corporal, I have been in the Corps four years—all four tangled up in one combat situation after another. None of them, as bad as they were, can compare to the one I am fighting in my head. I dropped out of college and joined the Marines to die, man, not to fight for my country or avenge 9/11. I joined for my own selfish reasons.

"I have always been selfish. Because I am big and strong and from a rich family, I have been treated with incredible favor, and I have sucked it up by the barrelful. I have never given back, not ever. I expected favors whenever I strutted down the halls at school and looked down my nose at the inferior masses who got in my way. Coaches loved me because I could play sports and win games. Mothers loved me because I smiled and said, 'Yes, ma'am, I will have your daughter back by ten o'clock,' when in fact all I wanted to do was bang premium ass and move on to the next conquest. When I got to Texas A&M, it was the same game, just higher stakes: more girls, more perks, more, more, and more.

"My joy was in pissing on people and seeing how much

humiliation I could inflict on anyone uglier, dumber, weaker, or less fortunate than me. I have been despised by most of the people in my life, and I didn't give a shit. I was a walking god, just one pathetic step away from narcissism, maybe not even a full step. I didn't do shit in college but play ball. I was catered to in every way. Hell, all the players were. We expected it. My life was disgusting and self-serving, and I just didn't give a shit. But that all changed one night, July 4, 1999." Blake's eyes were pools of agony as he looked at Briggs.

"I was on my way to the third party of the night with two of my buddies. We were all wasted drunk. My friend Peter was driving, Bart was in the passenger seat, and I was in the back. Peter said he had to pee, and he jerked the wheel hard in an attempt to turn on to a dirt road. The car spun. It skidded, crashed. Hello, tree. Peter was thrown from the driver's seat and into the dirt. I slammed into the left side of the back seat and broke my shoulder, but Bart took the brunt of the impact." Blake stopped and gulped, visibly shaking. "Bart smashed into the dashboard and the top of the windshield before he careened out the top of the convertible. His chest was ripped open. We could see his lungs and veins. His chest was sucking air through his exposed ribs and he was wheezing. And then, in a very weak voice he asked, 'What happened?'

"I just froze. To this day, I have never seen so much blood. To this very day.

"I turned around and saw Peter standing behind me, just as pale and shaking as I probably was. He kept saying, 'Oh God, oh God, oh God,' and I told him to shut the fuck up. Bart was somehow able to tell us to get the cell phone from his pocket. Shit, he even tried to take it out himself. He was torn to freaking pieces, man! I got the phone in my hand, feeling the pain in my shoulder for the first time, but I didn't care. When I started to dial 911, Peter took the phone out of my hand. At that very same moment, Bart started to convulse, spitting up blood. He was a goner, man. We knew it. I looked up at Peter, who just stood there holding the phone, and at that moment, I knew. I knew he was going to save his own ass, even if it cost Bart his.

"I sat there on the ground, holding Bart as the life faded from his body. Peter kept asking if he was dead yet. I . . . I couldn't speak. I couldn't move. It was as if I was outside of my body watching, not a part of it at all. I didn't want to be a part of it. Then, without a word, Peter dragged Bart's lifeless body from my arms and settled him in the driver's seat of the car. There was no conversation; we understood what the deal would be. Our friend would take the blame. I was overcome with complete disgust at Peter, but mostly at myself and the worthless, self-serving pile of shit I had become. I was disturbed and disgusted by how far down I had stooped in my young life."

Tears poured down Blake's face.

"So, man, this was the kind of despicable human being I had become. I hated myself from that moment on and have never stopped and never will until my life is over." With that, he fell back on his haunches, his shoulders hanging heavily.

Briggs positioned himself so that he could look Blake in the eyes. He waited until the Marine lifted his head.

"Blake, coming here to die is not the answer. Your place is back home with those you have hurt. You can find some comfort there, if you try."

Blake sniffed and wiped his nose with his shirt. "Peter found comfort at the end of a shotgun barrel one month after Bart was buried. The only thing that kept me from doing the same was seeing what it did to Peter's mother. She was crushed and never set foot outside her house. I didn't want my mother to do the same. On top of it all, Peter not only left his family, but his girlfriend was knocked up, so he left her and his child too. She blamed herself for

Peter's suicide, thinking that it was her fault because she wouldn't abort the baby."

Blake stared off into sights unseen by Briggs. Then in a clear and focused voice, he said, "Shit, I can't even catch a bullet or a decent piece of shrapnel. All my purple hearts are for scratches and broken bones. It's as if my payback for my horrendous sins will never end, never give me peace. You have no idea what it is like to hate yourself and not be able to put a bullet in your head. Man, for being the most dangerous place on earth, Iraq just isn't holding up its end of the bargain."

Blake wiped a final slew of tears from his face and chin as he stared down at the street.

He's staring down a hole of constant agony—no comfort, no hope, Briggs thought, realizing his own face was damp with tears. He quickly wiped them away.

Blake spoke again. "Eventually, my dad figured it all out. We didn't think about the logistics, how it would eventually come to light. Peter was already gone by then. It was just me. I can still see the despair in my dad's eyes when he told me he knew the truth—that I'd committed a vile crime against my friend, his family, and his memory.

"You know, he told me every day of my selfish life that he loved me and was proud of me. He showed me in every way that he supported me and would never let me down. He once told me that being a good son was all he ever expected of me and that all the touchdowns and good grades in the world meant nothing—all he wanted was a good and decent son who loved him equally in return.

"But I wasn't, and I didn't. All I ever cared about was status and what color BMW I would get each year. I never recognized the love my father had for me . . . not until that day, when I watched his demeanor turn cold and any feeling he had for me flushed from his eyes. I felt thrown away like a discarded coat. That's when I joined the Corps, hoping to die here in this cesspool of hate and despair, where I belong . . . and hopefully not hurt anyone again. But now I get it. I fully understand what my punishment is: to live."

———————

Later that night at the barracks, Blake got up in the quiet of dark to go outside where the heads were set up. On his way, he saw his bunkmate curled up in the far corner of the hall with his blanket, pillow, and weapon, sleeping soundly on the cool concrete floor.

Must have driven him out of the room again by screaming in my sleep, Blake thought apologetically.

Instead of hitting the head, he returned to his rack and dug into the bottom of his C-bag. He gently withdrew a tattered, green, Marine-issue logbook. Stained with sweat and dried blood, it was his confessional, the link between what had happened and his personal mission of suicide by war. The tattered pages chronicled his day-to-day life in alarming detail. Truths told one story at a time, like pennies for his sins. Maybe someday, someone would read it and would understand and forgive him.

On the upper left-hand corner of the book was a deep indentation from a bullet impact. The journal had kept the bullet from penetrating Blake's chest two years earlier in a firefight inside Fallujah. A ball round had struck it and stopped, then fell down between his shirt and skin, causing a nasty burn on his stomach. Small fragments of paper would flake off from the journal each time he opened it. That ball round should have been the end of him.

Still, here I am, Blake thought wryly.

He made his way outside into the night, the sky filled with countless stars. The beauty of the night sky defied the ugly face of hatred that he felt for himself. He marveled at that contrast. Life was so cheap, it seemed, taken quickly from so many. He sat down against the wall of the barracks and began to write. The night was so bright with ambient light that he didn't need his flashlight to see the pages.

He began his entry as he had done so many times before.

Dear Dad . . .

He waded into the day's events in alarming detail. He confessed to all the outrageous chances he had taken with total disregard for his own safety. How he had taken the lives of others in order to save his friends, about the dead Marines he helped drag out of firing zones, and how sorry he was about his life in general.

When his daily confession was complete, he closed the book and took out a standard Marine Corps letterhead. He wrote a short message to his family, just a few lines that always ended the same: "Love you all and will see you soon." These words were what he sent home every two weeks or so, not the pages of truth from the journal, which would be mailed to his dad after Blake's death. It already had an address and instructions written inside the cover for whoever got stuck with the sorry task of informing his family of his demise.

It was 2300—too early for breakfast, too late for dinner. *Maybe I can get some sleep out here*, Blake thought. He leaned his head back and took in the stunning array of stars gazing back at him. He discovered a rare moment of comfort in the dark desert sky.

As he marveled at the sky, he noticed a light was on in one of the small buildings in the compound. He decided to check it out and headed over to find Briggs at a table covered by several crumpled pages of stationary. Blake felt a moment of discomfort recalling how he had spilled his guts to Briggs about his useless life and vile sins, but he quickly dismissed the thoughts and stepped into the invisible armor he had built around his emotions.

"You're up late, Briggs."

"You too. Know where we can get a good cup of coffee?" Briggs asked as he kicked out a chair from the other side of the table and motioned with his head for Blake to have a seat. "Take a load off."

"Thanks. Can't help you with the coffee. Man, what I would do for a decent cup of joe. What are you up to? Writing home?"

"No, I'm writing a letter to the parents of Lance Corporal Packer; he caught the RPG this morning."

"I thought that was the lieutenant's job," Blake said.

"It is, but he was my Marine more than the lieutenant's, so I want to write one, too."

"But he was only with your platoon two days, same as me." Blake seemed baffled by Briggs's gesture.

"Yeah, but he was still one of mine. His parents need to know that he died not just in the line of duty but in the presence of his own, protecting his friends and standing tall for what he believed in. He didn't just *die*—he made a difference. He left his mark on this lousy world, and he saved my life. Only I can convey that to his parents because I was the last soul to see life in his eyes, which obligates me to bear witness to his bravery."

Blake leaned over the table to look at the letter and tapped it with his finger. "There wasn't much bravery. He caught an RPG and painted the walls and ceiling with his guts." Briggs knew Blake was entertaining himself by getting under Briggs's skin.

Briggs checked his patience. "No, Blake. That's how he died. It's how he lived that shows his courage and bravery. His bravery started the day he joined the Corps and became my brother—*your* brother, man. He was cut from the same cloth as you and me; he was family. His drill instructor became his father; his company commander, his mother; the Grinder where they practiced marching, his playground; and his rifle, his lover. All that is what led him to his last order, which he took from me, to stand his ground and protect you and me as we ascended that ladder well. His parents need to know that they are not just getting a form letter. They need to know about their son. They need to know that David A. Packer, Lance Corporal USMC, had my back and cared enough about his title to follow orders—orders that led to his demise in the line of duty. He died doing something that mattered and that had a profound impact on the lives of others." Briggs stopped short, inhaling deeply, and leaned back in his chair.

"But he's dead. I mean people die here; that's the business of war. He died in the line of duty doing his job. We have to get on with our jobs. Can't take any of this too much to heart, right?" Blake shrugged.

"You're wrong. The battle that took his life is over and in the past. What you do in the heat of battle is different from what you do when it's over, and *that* is what's missing in *your* life, Blake. I don't know how you missed it, but you have to learn it somehow, and fast."

With that, Briggs stood and turned away from the table.

"Learn what, Briggs?"

"Compassion, you dumbass." Briggs turned back around and quickly picked up a page of the letter. "Not in these scribbled words, but the compassion in your heart. It's the common glue that even barbarians understand, Blake. The tears that are shed by families when they lose a loved one are universal. Tears come in every language, and they mean the same thing. Someone is in agony over the loss of another human being, precious and irreplaceable." Briggs sighed. He placed the letter back on the table as he sat down again.

"You told me that you came here to die because of the guilt you felt over what you did or didn't do. You need to start asking yourself if the price you're paying to feel better is worth the price your parents are going to pay when they get one of these letters.

You're torturing your parents, not yourself, and that act will be complete when your father has to bury you. No parent should have to put their child in a grave, Blake." Briggs leaned toward Blake over the table.

"It's your job as a good son to take care of your parents. You have to go home and make this right. You have to see to it that they live long, happy lives before you do your duty and bury them at the end of their time. You say you want things to change, the pain to stop. Well, this is how it's done. Christ, man, stop being selfish and go home, ask for forgiveness, learn compassion. I'll damn well bet your father shows you some. From what you've told me, he sounds like a great man. Do something tough for a change and stop wimping out. Humble yourself to your father. Give him the chance to forgive you, Blake."

Blake swallowed the lump of pride in his throat and nodded. Without another word, he stood and exited the room.

CHAPTER NINE

December 2005

After his first deployment, Briggs was recognized for his ability as a leader, and the war needed leaders, especially when the old ones were being taken from the battlefield on stretchers. Briggs's promotion to sergeant just prior to his return home between combat tours came quickly.

Briggs's battalion arrived home a week before Christmas and was told to disappear until the first week of January 2006. That was when they were to begin workup training for their return to Iraq in July.

The flight home on a chartered airline jet was the first time Briggs could relax in months. The flight attendants were attractive and dressed in patriotic red, white, and blue. There were banners and "Welcome Home" signs scattered about the cabin, and the flight crew took the time to shake the hands of each and every Marine on board. It was a strange sensation for Briggs to return home among all the fanfare, but it was also a letdown because he knew that Anita would not be there to greet him. He tried as hard as he could to let her go, but it was like pulling a live oak tree out of a clay bank with his bare hands. Something so strong and beautiful that could withstand the strongest of tides and winds could not be moved by simple will.

In Iraq, Briggs could keep focused on the task at hand. Perhaps that focus was what got him promoted so quickly. On the flight home, his mind was filled with thoughts of his mom and sister. They were the only family he had. He missed them but knew they didn't need him to take care of them. His sister had a husband to take care of her and his mom was more than fine. The only reason she occasionally worked at the fish house was to fill her time and be around her daughter and son-in-law, especially since Scott was gone. Small shards of guilt for not being there burst into his thoughts before he reminded himself, *This is what sons do. They leave home and become men.*

The pilot announced over the intercom, "Feet dry. I would like to say on behalf of the flight crew, welcome home. We're all proud of you."

The returning heroes erupted in cheers of adulation for their country.

"Feet dry" was a term used by the flight crew when the aircraft was returning from a long flight over water and had safely arrived over land.

Briggs had given up his seat next to the window to another Marine; however, upon hearing that the aircraft was approaching land, he leaned as close to the window as possible in order to take in the magnificent spectacle of the green coastline. Green! It was an incredibly soothing color, the color of home. After spending months upon months in a country where the color of the landscape was a dull blend of brown grasses and beige-colored sand, this simple thing alone brought him enormous joy.

When the aircraft touched down on the runway at the Marine Corps Air Station at Cherry Point, North Carolina, the cheers once again erupted, even louder than before. When the doors were opened and the gangway was connected to the belly of the aircraft, the scent of home filled the cabin.

"Oh, man, do you smell that?" the Marine in front of Briggs blurted out as he made his way to the exit. He turned and flashed a wide, gleaming white smile. The grass along the edge of the runways had just been cut and the incredible fragrance floated into the open cabin door.

Briggs smiled in return. The sweet aroma of home floated on the air and found its way to the senses of those who had given so much of themselves for so many. *The perfect homecoming.* This simple, seemingly insignificant act was so powerful that it caused Briggs and several of the Marines around him to fight back tears.

When Scott saw his mom and sister in the crowd of smiling faces, a lump formed in his throat. He was home.

After a quick parade on base, the ride home seemed to fly by. When Scott and his family arrived, he found his home invaded by friends. Dozens of cars were parked on the lawn. Tables were covered in food. Although the temperature was in the mid-sixties, the winter sunshine was glaring in its brilliance.

"Hope you don't mind, but everyone insisted on throwing you a welcome home party," his mother said, smiling as she reached over the armrest of the car to pat him on the leg.

The truth about the whole thing was that he did mind and was not looking forward to confronting everyone. The forced smiles that he would have to offer up in return for his family and friends' attention was almost unbearable to him. At the same time he realized that it was more for his mother than anything else, so he pushed on and put on a good son face.

When Scott opened the car door, he was overwhelmed by the smell of freshly cooked seafood. And the people. A sea of arms reached out to hug him all at once.

Some of his best friends were there. And even though he knew she wouldn't be there, Scott found his eyes searching for Anita among the multitude of faces that paraded through the house and yard.

His biggest fear was how to avoid someone who wanted to

hear a war story. It wrenched his guts just thinking about what to say to avoid a conversation about war. They had no idea how utterly horrible it was, and the worst part was they didn't have the right to ask him anything about it.

The first person to get a hold of him was Mike Shepherd, and simultaneously his friend Gerald Shepherd, no relation to Mike but they both shared the same last name. Hence, they were called the Shepherd brothers—kind of an unexplainable thing in such a little town. The three of them had been inseparable in high school and kept each other in and out of trouble at the same time.

Mr. Rose grabbed him by the shoulder halfway to the house and spun him around for an embrace and a firm handshake. He was one of the finest boat builders on Harkers Island and helped Scott build his first rowboat when he was just twelve.

So many people, so many faces. Briggs did his best to indulge their questions, but all he wanted to do was slip away to the quiet and serenity of the waters' edge. He was not the same person they remembered and grew up with. His profession eroded away the joy that such a gathering like this should arouse in someone.

After everyone had left, Scott talked to his mother for a long time. They sat comfortably in the living room next to the large sliding glass doors that overlooked the bay. The conversation was mostly about life in general with no major sticking points, save one, Anita. Scott asked his mother if she had seen Anita lately.

"No, I haven't."

Scott was surprised by his mother's matter-of-fact and slightly curt reply. The wheels in his head started to spin. "Mom," he said, reaching out to her as she got up to go into the kitchen. "What is it, Mom?"

"Nothing," she responded, patting her hair and refusing to look him in the eyes.

"I shouldn't have brought it up," he mumbled.

She sighed and stopped at the kitchen doorway. "No, you should've. I know how important she is to you, son. I'm only concerned about you. I just don't want to see your heart broken again."

"What do you mean 'again'?"

His mother didn't respond until she had returned with two glasses of sweet tea. Sitting close to him, she looked deeply into his eyes. "Anita has a baby, Scott. Her name is Jean, but they call her Sweetie."

Scott felt as though someone had punched him in the gut, and he slumped back against the sofa.

"There's more," his mom continued. "Her husband accused her of cheating on him." She paused and inhaled deeply. "With you. He thinks the baby is yours."

"But I haven't been here," Scott protested.

"Scott, Anita's husband is selfish and shallow-minded, and his family is no better. In fact, his mother was the one to put the thought in his head about the legitimacy of his own daughter. She didn't like the fact that her blue-blooded son had diluted their family gene pool by marrying, in her words, 'a backwater hick with only a high school education.'" She stopped to sip her tea and catch her breath. Scott remained silent. "And before his mother could talk her son into getting rid of her, Anita had a baby. So his mother convinced him that Sweetie had to be your child."

"But it's not true," Scott whispered, staring out the glass doors. "We've never even had . . ."

She smiled sadly at him. "I know—not just because I trust you, but because Anita told me."

"You talked to her? When?"

"Almost every week since she separated from her husband and temporarily moved back home with her mother. Her mother and I are best friends, if you'll remember."

"Are they getting divorced?" It came out before Scott could stop himself.

"Now we are getting back to my point of me protecting you and your heart. You need to stay away from her. She is trying to make her marriage work. She says she loves her husband and is trying to make things right."

"It doesn't sound right to me."

"It's not for you to say or even question."

Scott shook his head. "Mom, she still loves me. She came to me after boot camp and hugged me, and she was crying."

"I know."

"Did she tell you that too?"

"No, I saw," she said, then waved her hand in the air. "Oh, don't look so surprised. I'm your mother. I'm allowed to spy."

He sat back and took a deep breath. "If I could've been stationed at Cherry Point, then I could have made it work."

His mother smiled and leaned toward him, placing her elbows on her knees. "No, you couldn't have. What has happened, what is happening, and what is going to happen are supposed to be. You have a strong will and so does she. If the two of you had managed to somehow change each other, it wouldn't have worked out either." She lowered her head in order to catch his gaze. "Only you can change yourself, and it is the same for Anita. Trust me, I've been around awhile. Give her time to fix her marriage. And you need to move on, for your own sake."

Scott nodded. He knew she was right, and he trusted her wisdom.

True to his word, to himself and his mother, he stayed clear of Anita, but it wasn't easy. Every day he had to fight the urge to travel the short distance down the road to Anita's house, and to do so, he needed every ounce of the discipline that his mother, his father, and his military training had taught him.

CHAPTER TEN

July 2006

Time passed quickly. He would have much rather spent July at home in Gloucester, North Carolina, but he knew that his return to Iraq would give his fellow Marines the opportunity to spend it with their loved ones. In that there was a great comfort. Each rise and fall of the full moon over the Outer Banks hastened along his return to Iraq. Once again it was his battalion's turn to relieve those who were on duty in Iraq. Fresh faces and old weathered faces with clean weapons and uniforms returned to relieve those who were tired, worn out, and dirty. He was back, and back in a place that he felt oddly familiar with and comfortable in. All of the combat experienced Marines felt the same way. This was their job; it was what they were trained to do.

Briggs and Blake were part of a small unit performing a recon mission in Baghdad when a young boy ran out and grabbed Briggs by his arm, pulling him toward a building as he shouted in Arabic.

"Hey, hold up, kid. Ashie, what's this kid saying?"

Ashie was a terp—an interpreter. He'd been with Briggs's platoon for three months and knew damn near everyone.

"He says he knows where the Marine we are looking for is, but we have to hurry. They are moving him."

"He must be talking about Adams," Briggs shouted to Blake.

Two days prior, Lieutenant Adams had been part of a contingent of four Humvees and eleven Marines who daily escorted children to school. When the Humvee rounded the corner of a block-long street surrounded by four-story buildings and burned-out shops, the enemy had opened fire. Lieutenant Adams had been riding in the passenger seat of the first Humvee when an IED went off behind him, blowing the small bus full of children over on its side and spilling them into the streets. Adams had been hit by sniper fire, grabbed by two of the enemy, and thrown into a waiting truck. He had been missing for approximately thirty-six hours.

"Blake, call it in right now," Briggs yelled as he assembled the five men with him and took off following the kid. He hollered over his shoulder, "He's not leading us into a slaughter, is he, Ashie?"

Ashie struggled to keep up with Briggs at full run. "No, I know his parents and family. He is a good boy. He goes to school."

The boy kept a brisk pace. As the men followed, the rattling of their gear and stomping boots broadcasted their arrival around each corner and down every alleyway.

"Okay, okay. Stop him," Briggs ordered Ashie after five minutes of running. "Get him over here and ask him where this place is before we get too close. I don't want to run up on top of their lookouts."

Ashie conveyed Briggs's request to the boy, who said that he and his two cousins were the lookouts and that there were no others that he knew of. He told them they were close to the hideout. Suddenly, a small pickup full of men sped by, almost hitting Briggs and Ashie as it careened around the corner.

"Guns, guns, guns!" Blake yelled.

"Shit! Cover!" Briggs screamed, recognizing the threat as he quickly started mowing down the six men who'd jumped from the back of the truck with their automatic weapons. The insurgents never had a chance. All were hit several times, some before they even had their feet on the ground. Two other Marines put over one hundred SAW rounds directly into the truck in just a few seconds, giving Briggs and Ashie a chance to hit the ground in order to clear fire. The automatic fire from the two SAWs was devastating. The insurgents' bodies danced in the air, jerking and twitching, as multiple rounds of ball and tracer fractured their bones and flesh, ripping them apart and spraying blood in a cascade of red mist into the air. They fell with a flop to the ground.

As the smoke from the ricocheting rounds cleared, a small red truck came crashing around the corner. Two were in the front of the truck, two in the back bed. The two in the back jumped down and dashed toward a building. Briggs leveled his weapon on them and loudly ordered them to stop. They turned their weapons toward him just before they entered the flimsy building and opened fire in his direction.

To Briggs's left, Blake and Ninja opened fire on the driver and passenger, who tried to turn inside the cab of the small truck and aim their weapons. The driver, seeing they were in no position to shoot, punched the gas and tried to speed away. Too late. Blake dropped to one knee and blazed a perfectly straight line of automatic fire that swept the cab of the truck from left to right. The windows shuddered and both men slumped over. The truck bounced off the corner of a building and crashed into a pile of rocks and rubble.

Unflinching, Briggs stood his ground as the chain and spent rounds fell at his feet and bounced off his boots. He directed his attention to the insurgents who were running by the building. Two quick pulls of the trigger. Briggs followed the rounds as they left the barrel of his rifle and ripped into the first man's chest. The two men were lined up and Briggs knew that at least one of the bullets would pass through the first man and hit the other. His aim and concentration were flawless.

Now wait, just wait, Briggs thought. Fractions of a moment passed like minutes. The first man completed his fall, exposing the second man to a fatal shot. Briggs saw a small red spot on the second man's shirt just under his right elbow. He snapped off two more rounds. The man stumbled into the building and fell to the floor. Briggs darted toward the first man, who lay motionless. *Definitely dead.* Briggs stood on the barrel of the dead insurgent's weapon and covered the door.

"Blake!" he barked. "In."

Blake rushed into the building and covered the second man on the floor, ensuring he was dead and not just laying in wait to kill them.

"Clear," he yelled back.

"Hey Sarge, you had better check this out," Ninja hollered from the street. "There is someone rolled up in a rug in the back of this truck."

"Blake, check out that building! Make sure it's clear."

"It's good."

"Set up a perimeter, from here to here." Briggs swept his hand around the front of the street. All the calls came back clear.

"Hey, this dude is speaking English, Sergeant." Ninja was poking the rug with his rifle barrel.

"Don't do that shit, Ninja. Paco, help him get that guy out of there."

Lance Corporal Tim Lawrence, known as Ninja, was the company clown. He would do anything for a laugh, especially when he had a six-pack in him. He only weighed one hundred and thirty-five pounds, and that was after a heavy breakfast. His father owned a large bar and grill somewhere in New Jersey. That was where he discovered his talent for drinking too much beer and acting like a fool. One month before his first deployment, he donned a cape and ski mask and jumped off a fence at the back of the squad bay, he earned a broken leg and the nickname Ninja. He was not able to go overseas with his unit until the next deployment.

Despite his reputation as a clown, Ninja was incredibly disciplined when it came to fulfilling his duties on patrol. He never had to be told twice to do anything. Briggs assumed it was from the guilt he felt after he missed his first deployment and three of his best friends didn't come home.

Briggs was approaching the truck where Paco stood near the rolled-up rug. "Who the hell are you, man?" Paco shouted.

The voice came back muffled and excited. "I am Lieutenant Adams, USMC."

"No shit." Paco pulled away the rug and uncovered the man's head. "Sergeant, you'd better get over here. I think we found our guy."

"Get him over here, Paco. Now!" Briggs shouted as he motioned toward the building.

"He's a little shot up, Sergeant, but I don't think we did it. I know I didn't do it."

"Shut up and get him in this building."

Lance Corporal Mark Pacachellie, a.k.a., Paco, did as he was told and threw the wounded lieutenant over his shoulder and ran into the building. He put him down on the floor next to the dead insurgent. Blood covered his hands from a wound on the lieutenant's leg.

"Man, this ain't good," Paco said. "We could get our asses killed in here. We need help now, Sergeant."

Pacachellie was serving his first tour in Iraq. He was from New York City with a strong city accent and very Italian in appearance. His hair was Elvis black, and he always looked like he needed a shave, even right after he'd shaved. He embraced his nickname of Paco and joked with everyone that he was half-Spanish on his mother's side.

Briggs could see Paco starting to freak. He replied firmly, "No one is going to die until it's time to die and today ain't the day. Now shut up and cover that window."

"Man, this is fucked up. We need help. We got to get help." Paco was vigorously wiping the blood from his hands onto his pant legs. He shifted his weapon back and forth by squeezing it under his arm, clearly getting more and more frustrated.

"Listen to me, damn it." Briggs gripped Paco's shoulder. "You got two choices, man. Either you do your job and fall back on your training and help all of us, or you freak out and die, here, now, in this shithole. One thing is for sure: anyone who keeps his head and follows orders will make it out of here. Now act like a Marine and pick up that damn SAW. Snap out of your cheap shit and do your job."

Paco took a deep breath and glanced at the dead insurgent at their feet. Briggs pulled him close and whispered, "Trust me. I will get us out of this, okay?"

"Okay, Sergeant." Paco took a deep breath and checked his weapon.

Paco moved back to the window with a calmness that let Briggs know that Paco was back on board and in control of his emotions. Briggs sighed with relief. He needed to count on all of them to do their jobs, and he knew that if they did, real heroes would emerge, doing extraordinary things in extraordinary circumstances.

Sitting in the burned-out building, its mortar barely holding it together after being shaken to its limits by RPGs, grenades, and small arms, Briggs gazed over at Lieutenant Adams with concern. The bandage covering the wound on his leg was totally soaked through.

"Lieutenant," Briggs said quietly as he extended his hand with a fresh dressing. "Scoot over here and let me put this over the top of that one and tighten it up."

"Yeah, I didn't do such a good job, did I?" Adams slid over to Briggs's side, dragging his leg. "Damn, that hurts, but at least it's a through-and-through."

Briggs rolled him over to get a good angle to reach around his leg. "Yep, it looks that way. When did this happen?" Briggs tightened the first of two straps that would secure the bandage and slow the bleeding.

"The very first day I was with the contingent escorting the kids, and—get this—the very first shot. I think it was a sniper. Good thing he was a shitty shot. All hell broke loose. I came to a short time later, and a corpsman was putting this dressing on me. Damn, there were a lot of bullets flying. He had me just inside a doorway, leaning over me. I was just about to ask him about my wound when his head exploded in my face. Someone inside the building stuck a rifle barrel in his face and let him have it. That's when I got grabbed. I guess they thought I would look good on one of their videos."

Briggs knelt beside the lieutenant. "So what brought you to this train wreck of a country?" he asked, trying to make the lieutenant feel better and keep his mind off his wound and their perilous situation. Briggs placed his hand on Adams's neck to check his temperature and to see if he was in shock.

"No good reason really. I don't have anything else in my life. Just me. It's always been that way. One foster home after another, no real love in between. Foster parents aren't really parents, just someone the state pays to board you. Love and compassion are buried deep in the fine print of the contract, never catching air. I always knew I was just a paycheck. So around the age of thirteen, I knew I had to get out of the spinning toilet of foster care, but

I managed to screw that up by pissing off my third set of foster parents and landing my ass in a cattle barn."

"What the hell is a cattle barn?" Briggs rose to look out the window, studying the street.

"Basically it's a house with several bedrooms and a wrangler, or responsible adult, to make sure you're in bed on time."

Briggs nodded, still looking out the window. "So what happened?"

"So I started hanging out at a recruiting station less than a block from where I was living. This staff sergeant sort of took me under his wing—you know, not running me off—and he really made me feel like I belonged there. I never felt that way before. I soon found that it *is* normal to feel like you belong somewhere, and that feeling led me to hope. I never felt that before either. After that, all I could think of was graduating high school and going into the Corps. I used to be nothing but a screw-up with no motivation, but when that staff sergeant told me I couldn't get into the Marines if I didn't finish high school or if I had a record, that was it.

"It was almost a miracle how I turned it around—got straight As, stopped hanging with thugs, and stopped the drugs. It was the most powerful thing that ever happened to me, you know? Someone really caring for me. Looking back, the reality of it is that the staff sergeant was just another fast-talking snake oil salesman, lining up his next sale, but hey, it worked for me. I made my way through a few enlisted ranks and then got into college on an officer program. ROTC, TBS, all that, and here I am paying back my time to the Corps so I can get out."

"What's next?"

"Well, when I get out next year, I'm going back to school to get my master's in finance. I have this weird notion that I would like to be a stockbroker or in banking, something nutty like that. Beats getting shot at."

"Yeah, it does," Briggs replied.

"What's your story, Sergeant?"

"My story is much less complex than yours, sir."

"So give it up."

"It'll have to wait, sir." Briggs stood and turned to his man at the front of the room. "Blake, is that street still clear on your end?"

"Still clear, Sergeant."

"Paco?"

"Still clear here too, Sergeant."

"Blake, did you get that radio call out?"

"Yeah, I did. Sergeant, they know we are in trouble, but they're also fighting on the other end of town. Same kind of thing going on there."

"Okay. How bad did we shoot up that second truck?"

"The red one, Sergeant?" asked the young corporal on the second SAW.

Briggs nodded.

"Not too bad. I didn't see it blow up or anything."

"One of the front tires is out, Sergeant," Paco chimed in.

Briggs cursed under his breath. "Okay, here is the plan. I'm going to get that truck and bring it around. Cover me on the way out. If it runs, I'm coming back, and I mean *back*. I'm going to bring it through the front of this building ass first, so stay away from the front walls. When you see it moving this way, call in to base and tell them we're coming down road Bravo in this piece of shit and not to shoot at us, got it? Once I'm in, you all jump in the back and get as far in the back of the truck as you can, especially on the driver's side. That will help take the weight off the front right tire. It's the only way I will be able to steer that thing. Blake, you and Ninja are on the lieutenant—push him all the way to the front of the bed." He looked at Adams and added, "Sorry. This might hurt a little."

Adams lifted his head. "Not a problem. I'm getting used to being thrown in the back of a truck. I can hang."

"I want one SAW shooting front and one covering back. Ninja left, Blake right. Are we clear?" Briggs took a moment to catch every eye in the room. Their response was affirmative.

He turned to Ashie. "That puts you in the front with me. I think that truck crashed on the right side, so be ready to jump in through the window if the door doesn't work, okay?"

Ashie nodded and smiled, giving a thumbs-up. "That's the way I like it. John Wayne-style, like a real cowboy."

"Yeah. Go get 'em, cowboy." Briggs raised his fist and bumped it against Ashie's. "Okay, check weapons and get ready."

Briggs stood and cleared the door. He immediately drew fire from street level and could see three men screaming and trying to gain cover. Their faces registered surprise when Briggs came running through the door. They were quickly dispatched by Ninja and Blake as a symphony of SAW fire flamed out of the windows of the building. The insurgents fell in their tracks without a twitch.

Briggs was less than forty yards from the truck. The entire street now knew his men were holed up in that building. He moved quickly and arrived at the driver's side door. There were two bodies in the front seat that needed to be discarded. The man in the driver's seat was already hanging halfway out; one quick jerk and he fell into the street. The man's weapon sat next to the corpse in the passenger seat.

As Briggs finished kicking out the shattered windshield, he noticed that the truck was still running. *What a wonderful sound.* Briggs slammed the truck into reverse and the tires squealed as he sped backward down the street. To his relief, he didn't drawn any other fire as he crashed through the plywood wall of the building.

"Okay . . . in, in, in. Let's go!" Briggs yelled.

Ashie managed to pull open the banged-up passenger side door, and he ejected the dead man from his seat with little effort.

"Let's go, cowboy," Ashie announced as he slammed the door.

Looking back, Briggs could see that everyone was ready. All the angles were covered and Ashie had his AK thrust through the empty windshield space. He could hear the lieutenant moaning.

Briggs flipped the gear into drive and rocketed away from the area, fast and clean. Ashie gave directions, turn for turn, down almost-empty streets back to base, back to the relative safety of the Green Zone, the only home they had right now with a bed and a hot meal. Even though it would only take five minutes to get there, the streets held danger around every corner. The smell of burning rubber was strong and the sound of screeching steel pierced the air as sparks flew down the side of the truck.

"We did it! We are almost home." Ashie reached over and slapped Briggs on the shoulder. "Damn, Briggs, you're bleeding." He pointed to Briggs's arm.

Briggs looked down briefly. "Yeah, I know. I think I caught a stray SAW round off one of the walls."

"Let me look," Ashie said as he reached over.

"No!" Briggs snapped. "Cover the road, Ashie. There will be time for that when we get home." He grabbed his friend's shoulder and shook it, then gave him a half smile. "Don't worry, brother. I won't die on you today. Remember, I said no one dies today."

Ashie returned a quick smile, then shook his head. "Okay, cowboy. Okay."

CHAPTER ELEVEN

August 2006

"How long are you going to be on medical leave?" Blake asked as he watched Briggs pack his bags.

"With a little luck, thirty days, even though I don't need it. It's not that bad of a wound. I'm just a little sore, more than anything. I will be back before you have a chance to miss me." Briggs had a sly grin on his face. "You sure you can handle the squad, Sergeant?"

"I'm not a sergeant yet, Sergeant."

Briggs opened his palm to reveal a set of sergeant chevrons. "You'll need these. The company commander is going to promote you in the morning at muster. Sorry I won't be there. I have to leave tonight. So here." He held them out to Blake, encouraging him to take them. "At least your first set will come from me."

"You're shitting me!" Blake's eyes were wide as he picked up the chevrons. "I'm not due for this promotion for six more months." He stared at the chevrons in disbelief.

"So you're happy about this?"

"Hell yes, I'm happy! This is a big deal. I . . . I don't know what to say."

"Say you will take good care of my squad, and Ashie too. Those are my men, and I want them back in one piece." Briggs held out his hand and Blake shook it enthusiastically.

"You got it, Sergeant." Blake's grin was as big as it could possibly be.

Briggs smiled and pointed at Blake. "You have come a long way, Blake. Man, you really stepped up." He scratched his head and added, "Be careful."

Walking to the truck that would take him to the airport, Briggs thought of his mom. She would be waiting for him with open arms and a kitchen that was warm from the day's cooking. The table would be full of fresh seafood, dressed up with love from his mother's hands. His family would be there. They would arrive long before he did to help orchestrate the feast. They would all have something to contribute to the table: fresh flounder plucked from the shallows of the last full moon night; steamed oysters and clams piled on the table in small hills; blue crabs bigger than the palm of your hand; and beer so cold it froze your fingers as you fished it out of the bottom of the ice chest.

That was home.

And this homecoming would be the sweetest of all. Anita would be there to greet him.

To his surprise, he'd received a letter from Anita one month after his arrival back in country, bundled up with one of his mother's. She wrote that she missed him and was sorry for the way things had worked out. She was now divorced and asked if it would be all right for her to write to him and hoped it would not be awkward. She also said that she understood if he did not want to speak to her anymore.

Even though he had been deeply hurt by Anita, Briggs jumped at the chance to have her in his life again. He knew his Marine buddies would tell him he was being foolish, so he kept her letter to himself. That very same day, he'd written back, telling her she was still his one true love and writing to her would be the greatest thing in the world for him.

They'd exchanged letters every week, and in the last letter, he received a picture of Anita and young Sweetie sitting in the sunshine on the dock behind his house. He kept it in his pocket wherever he went, this image of the girl he loved and the beginnings of a family. It made Briggs think about how he wanted his life to be.

On the plane, he let in thoughts of home and how precious the memories of that place, and the people there, were to him. Existing in a place like Iraq had therapeutic value, but the desire of a simpler life without someone shooting at him had become quite attractive. He even thought about going to college. Catching a formal education looked better than catching bullets. Briggs's brief encounter with Lt. Adams had sparked in him a thought that made a lot of sense. College didn't seem like a bad idea. It was definitely better than boot blisters, crappy food, and the overwhelming opportunity to die in a country that didn't want him there in the first place.

Briggs's plane was scheduled to arrive at Cherry Point Marine Base at 1430 sharp. He thought it would never get there. Sitting for so long with nothing to do but think was hard. He changed the dressing on his arm and used a smaller, less obvious one. This wasn't the first time he had come home shot up, and he knew it worried his mother. He would try to downplay his injuries, as always, but he also knew that it would be the first thing she would ask about and demand to inspect.

Briggs was on a flight with another Marine unit returning home at the end of its deployment. The excitement inside the cabin of the chartered 747 was familiar; however, it had little effect on Briggs. He felt alone. His excitement was contained only in his thoughts of seeing Anita. And that alone helped suppress the guilt he felt for not being with his friends in his unit. As the wheels of the aircraft touched down and rolled to a stop, "Welcome Home" banners could be seen strewn along the fences of the airfield. The entire flight line was swollen with family and friends as far as the chain-link fence would reach.

For each Marine on the plane, the sight lifted hearts and spirits to heights woefully lacking in the territories of battle.

The Marine he was sitting next to said, "Man, it's good to be home." Briggs agreed with a slight nod of his head, because speaking would only reveal the emotions he was trying so hard to keep in check.

The plane landed and he stepped onto the tarmac, closed his eyes, and inhaled deeply.

Yes, this is home.

Anita was the first to reach him, catching him off guard. She embraced him tightly, burying her face into his chest. He wrapped one hand around her body and the other held her head tenderly. He kissed the top of her head, welcoming the scent and feel of her, a woman now, but still his girl.

Oh my god! There you are. Briggs thought to himself as he embraced her. She seemed so small to him, so delicate and vulnerable. For that moment everything stopped, there was no sound, there was no color, and there was no motion. He froze the moment in his mind so that he would remember it forever. I don't want this to stop. I don't want to let go of her. He refused to let the fear and doubt of the moment falling apart to enter his mind.

"I'm so glad you're home," she said as she started to cry.

Then the hugs kept coming, next from his mother, then his sister, then his brother-in-law, and then his friends, each waiting their turn to welcome him home. Eventually the circle around him ran three deep. It humbled him to the core, and he swiped at the tears which ran steadily now—the embattled, tough Marine completely melted by his hometown welcome.

"Where do we pick up your bags?" his mother asked.

"This is it, just this small bag. I don't need much where I've been." He gave her a half smile, and she smiled back, wrapping her arms around him again.

"Welcome home, my son."

He buried his head in his mother's neck. "It's good to be home, Mom." His voice cracked a bit when he added, "I wish I could express to you just how good it is."

Anita stood quietly next to him as he continued to greet his loved ones, but would occasionally gently reach out to touch his hand, his shoulder, and his back, as if claiming him for herself. At least, he hoped she was.

Anita and Scott did not speak much on the way back to the house; they were just content to be near each other. Everyone else was cackling like geese. The only real conversation Scott had was with his mother. She asked how long he would be home, and he told her almost the entire month. That was when it struck him as odd—he'd never heard of anyone spending so much time at home on convalescent leave for such a minor injury. Most of his friends only had ten days, a maximum of twenty. Well, chalk it up to good luck, he thought. Either way, he would take it.

The three-car procession with the minivan leading the way made it to Gloucester in less than forty minutes. A feast was on the table, just as he'd predicted, but the crowd seemed to have doubled compared to when he'd last returned home. There were more people, more cars, and even more boats tied up at the dock outside their home. Many he remembered from the last party, but others were just a blur from his past.

As Scott emerged from the car, applause erupted from the group. He started shaking hands and moving toward the house, and as he did, people patted him on the back, shoulders, and head. He stopped just short of the driveway and held up his hands. The symphony of voices and applause died down just enough for Scott to make a quick speech.

"Man, you people will do anything to get out of the house," he said in a jovial manner. "Thank you, thank all of you, for coming to see me and welcoming me home. But the truth is I know you're all here for the food, so don't let me stop you."

Amidst the laughter, the guests began to settle around the tables. An old family friend hollered out, "That's right! It's all about the food!" and another roar of laughter followed.

Everyone wanted to shake his hand and thank him for his service to their country. He was overwhelmed and humbled by their gratitude, though he secretly hoped as the day wore on that he would not be bombarded with questions about the war. He wanted to put that behind him for now. More than anything, he wanted to spend his time with Anita—and maybe get in a little fishing.

After the meal, he changed into his shorts and a Big Rock fishing tournament T-shirt. The crowd had diminished and a small group of women from church were cleaning up tables on the front lawn. Anita was patiently waiting for him in the living room, sitting on the couch and gazing out the back window toward Brown's Island. He bent down and gently took her hand, lifted her from the couch, and embraced her.

There was a taste in his mouth from long-ago memories. Memories of his first kiss, his best kiss, his last kiss. The memory held his hopes of renewing his relationship with the giver of that kiss. He thought that kiss was lost to him forever, never again to be tasted. But love was not realistic, and neither was Scott when it came to Anita. He harbored hope, and in hope, there was no loss. He hoped she would belong to him again. He spoke the words he had longed to say for a long time.

"I know I told you this in my letters, but I wanted to say it to you again in person. I love you, Anita. I always have, and I always will."

She started to tear up again and he wanted something more than tears between them, so he kissed her. And it blew his mind. He felt as though the magic between them was finally speaking to each other's hearts. Her warm, soft body pressed against his like a puzzle piece fitting perfectly. He knew—as he'd always known— that they were meant to be together, just as sunlight was meant to bathe in the ocean. He drew back from her and looked into her eyes, which were brimming with tears until one finally spilled over. She giggled and he smiled, wiping that tear away with his hand. She gently laid her hand on his injured arm.

"Does it hurt still?" she asked, tenderness in her voice.

"Hm. Only when you press on it like that."

"Oh!" she said, and pulled her hand away quickly, her eyes wide. When she caught on to his teasing, she made a tsk sound and slapped him on the other arm.

"You're so bad," she said, giggling lightly.

"Not so bad," he said softly.

Then she gazed deeply into his eyes, smiling her intoxicating smile with her luscious full lips, and he became lost in her. His heartbeat quickened and he had to remember to breathe. The power of the moment was exhilarating.

He led her through the back door into the late afternoon sun, hand in hand, knowing if he didn't get out of the house, he would have led her to his old room and closed the door for a long, long time.

It was peaceful there in the shallows, where the flat-bottom boats and the Down-easter's gently jostled with the wind, begging to fish. Scott and Anita stood at the end of the dock and soaked in the moment. He felt at peace for the first time in months.

After a while, Charley, Scott's old friend, and the Shepherd brothers broke the silence as they walked along the dock. Charley was wearing shin-high white rubber boots, lovingly referred to as "Harker's Island house slippers." His sunburned face was the product of a successful shrimping season, and his stained white T-shirt an expression of his gratitude for a feast well served.

"We are going to hit the flatfish tonight. You up for it, bro?"

"Maybe tomorrow," Scott said with a tired smile. His friends nodded, winked, and walked back along the dock.

The party was rapidly drawing to a close as more and more people left to return to their homes and leave the Briggs family to privately enjoy their reunion. The hordes of people that enjoyed the party helped clean up the grounds and put away all the dishes. There was little left to do so Scott's mother ventured out with some friends to return home later that evening.

Scott and Anita made their way to the heavily wooded area of the property along the water's edge. It was a place they would be unseen by anyone so that they could share a private moment.

Scott leaned into Anita and ran his hand up the back of her neck. Although she had left him for someone else and had had a child with another man, Scott didn't give Anita's past a second thought. He had her now, and if that was how it needed to play out for him to have her, then he was okay with that. More than okay.

They turned their attention to the setting sun, and Scott broke the silence.

"When my enlistment is up, I'm going to get out," he said in a calm voice, rubbing the top of her hand with his thumb. He pulled her to him, then spun her around to face the setting sun. He wrapped his arms around her waist.

"I've decided to go to college and get a good job, one where people aren't shooting at me," he whispered in her ear.

She spun back around to look at him, her eyes wide with

excitement. "Oh, Scott, that's wonderful!" She held his face in her hands. "What do you want to do? What school are you going to attend?"

"Whoa, whoa, not so fast. I'm a long way off from making those decisions. I'll figure it all out as I go along. Whatever I decide to do, I want to make sure I'll be close to home."

"Home," she said with a widening smile.

"Yes, home. You were right. This is my home. I have seen a few places and I'm sure this is the place for me. Dodging bullets," he lifted his injured arm, "or more like catching bullets, has gotten old."

"Scott, you don't know how happy that makes me. We don't need anything more than this."

He assumed she was talking about the love the two of them shared, but she turned to face the bay and spread out her arms. "All of this," she whispered. Her fingertips were extended and separated so that the setting sun shone through them, flickering yellow and solid ribbons of gold.

He stepped back to take her in. Her slender body, so strong and yet so feminine, was perfectly centered in front of the sinking sun. She tossed her head back and spun in a tight circle. Her long strands of silky, blonde hair floated away from her shoulders and face. She completed one last spin and collided with him, pulling him down onto the lush green grass by the dock, straddling his hips.

"Oh, I'm so sorry, I forgot about your arm. Did I hurt you?" Anita covered her mouth with her hand and gazed down at his smiling face.

Scott let out a laugh so loud he was certain he could be heard all the way to the house. "The pain has been gone for a long time now, especially with you in my arms."

"Are you sure?"

"Yes, I'm sure. My arm feels great, almost like it never happened. Look." He held up his right arm, flexing his biceps. It bulged, firm and large. Anita squeezed it.

"Oh, yes, I see what you mean. My big, strong Marine." Her smile revealed perfect white teeth.

Briggs lay beneath her as she sat upright and straight on top of him. He marveled at the way her hair floated back down to her shoulders and settled perfectly around her face. The backdrop of the sun danced across each errant strand still falling into position. She quickly changed from seriously intoxicating to impulsively seductive. She leaned forward and kissed his forehead, then on each side of his face. She gently touched her full, lush lips across his and lightly ran the tip of her tongue inside his mouth, beneath his upper lip. Starting at her thighs, Scott ran his hands up her sides, brushing her firm breasts with his thumbs and then in unison over her shoulders to the back of her head. He gathered up her hair in his hands and pulled her lips to his. She emitted a sound from deep within her core that vibrated from her throat as it escaped her lips.

Anita placed her hands on Scott's chest, one on top of the other. She pushed away from him, arching her back, and lightly shook her head, allowing her hair to fall behind her shoulders and gather in the middle of her back.

"You are a goddess," he exhaled. He placed his hands on her knees and then her hips. She untied the two strings that held up her sundress, and slowly, tauntingly, extended them as far as they would reach, holding up the ends with her fingertips. She paused with her arms stretched over her head. It felt like eternity. She let them fall. Her dress draped down, revealing the top of her magnificent breasts. They were full and firm, perfect in proportion. Scott dared not move a muscle. He reveled in her perfectly orchestrated ballet of seduction. And he knew she could feel just how appreciative he was of her efforts through the straining fabric of his pants.

She leaned forward once more and placed a tender kiss on his forehead, barely touching his skin. Then another, and another. Small beads of sweat popped up on his cheeks and neck. Scott let out a moan of surrender. He and Anita had been this far before and had always stopped.

Anita sat up, still straddling him, and gazed down as he lay helpless, his eyes barely open, swimming in the euphoria of their encounter.

"You're so beautiful, and I'm so lucky," he gasped, barely able to speak. "There isn't a prettier girl on this earth."

The light was quickly fading behind her. The orange and yellow of the sun softened the edges around her silhouette.

"We're missing the sun taking its evening bath. It's shedding its clothing of bright colors and dripping down into the ocean before it sleeps," she said.

"Very poetic, but I would rather watch you," Scott whispered. He ran his hands over her waist, his thumbs once again barely touching the sides of her breasts as he slid his hands up to her shoulders. The top of her sundress still dangled loosely over her tanned breasts, almost revealing the dark brown flesh of her hardened nipples. Anita pulled at the sundress, slowly revealing a fraction more of herself, then another, until the cotton fabric caught on her taut nipples. And that was the limit of his patience.

"Come here." Scott placed his hands on either side of Anita's face. He gently drew her close to him and kissed her softly on her lips. At the same time, he reluctantly pulled up the strings of her dress and attempted to tie them back. As much as he wanted her, right there and then, he wanted her to know that it wasn't just her body he wanted—he wanted all of her.

"Don't forget my promise," Scott whispered in her ear.

"I remember your promise. It was the sweetest thing you have ever said." She smiled as though she was thinking of herself as the ten-year-old girl that Scott had asked to be his girlfriend. Only if you promise to marry me one day, she had responded, and he had promised with all his heart. Thus their love had begun.

Being married to Anita was, and had been, his dream for years. They had talked about marriage in the past, but it was not the right time now. When he asked her that all-important question, everything had to be right.

"Scott, it's okay. I want you badly."

"And I want you but I will keep my promise of virginity until we're married. I'll keep this promise to you, to us, and most importantly, to me."

Scott rolled her over onto the grass and brushed the hair from her face.

"One of the reasons I love you so much is that you allow me to keep this promise," he said. With that, he stood and walked to the edge of the grass where the sandy shore met the bay. He stood there in the falling darkness, staring intently out across the water.

He heard Anita stand, tie her top, and approach him. "That's why I love you, Scott. You know, it's hard to find a good man, especially one that keeps his word, even though it's extremely difficult to do so sometimes."

"Oh, trust me. It's extremely hard, I mean, to do so, you know . . . to keep my word. And my pants on for that matter."

Reluctant to end their reunion, they stood hand in hand, watching the sun kissing the waters of the Outer Banks. The bay was wide, interrupted only by the dark edges of Brown's and Harkers Islands, where the water married with the sandy shorelines planted with cord grass and live oaks.

"What's it like to kill someone?"

Momentarily, he was stunned. "Boy, talk about a change of subject," he said, trying to make light of the very question he would rather die than answer.

Anita leaned into him, wrapped her arms around him, and pressed her cheek against his shoulder. "I'm sorry."

Scott gently touched her face as he thought about how to answer her question. "No, it's okay. I understand why you ask. It's just that most of the time, the Marines who haven't seen combat ask that question as if it's a point of entertainment. 'So how many guys you kill, Sarge?' Like I'm going to break into a song and dance for them." He looked at her and tilted his head. "But I know you don't mean it that way. Still, it's a damned question."

Scott stepped away from her and inched closer to the edge of the sandy beach. *This ocean at my feet is the answer to her question. The water is unpredictable and chaotic, changing constantly, capable of both creation and destruction. It just depends on the circumstance.*

The dark splashing waves slapped themselves into a white foam that quickly faded back to black as the next ushered in. Anita wrapped her arms around him from behind.

"I'm so sorry. I never should have asked you that. It's probably something I don't want to know anyway, and I don't want to bring up painful memories."

"No, it's okay." Scott stood still and drew in a long deep breath. "There's just not an easy answer, is all." The smell of the sea air intermingled with her perfume and gave him comfort, comfort enough to share with her something far more intimate than any sexual encounter. He trusted this woman with all things, and so he would trust her with the battering ram of emotions he felt whenever he was placed in a position to kill.

"Someone far wiser than me once told me I have to talk to someone I trusted about this. I have to share my sin."

"Sin? But you're fighting a war and in combat."

"Yes, that's true, but bear with me. This man told me I should share my sin with another whom I trust or it would consume me a little at a time." He turned and embraced her, then lightly kissed her on the forehead.

Scott knew that the evening had to end because Anita needed to return home in order to take over the duties of watching Sweetie from her mother. The process of introducing Scott into their lives would not be difficult, but it had to be done properly. The party had been a wonderful distraction where Anita was able to ease Sweetie into the relationship without directly placing Scott into her life.

Sweetie would probably be fast asleep when Anita got home because she spent most of the day running and playing in the yard with the other young children her age. She was such a wonderful sight to see, young and happy in a knee-high cotton sundress and her long flowing yellow hair trailing behind her as she gleefully ran from tree to tree and person-to-person. Her wide inviting smile glowed of honesty and wonder. The entire time Sweetie was there she was distracted by all the different people and the vigilant eye of her mother and grandmother. For all she knew it was just a nice party down the street where she could run and play with her friends. Scott was willing to take it slow and be patient because he intended to be a part of their lives forever.

"Come on," he said as he walked toward the picnic table in the center of the yard. The wind was blowing just enough to keep down the mosquitoes. He led Anita to the old wooden table, stained with years of use from rain, barbecue sauce, and the occasional overturned drink. Shades of gray and dark brown kept it camouflaged, even with a hint of the porch light casting out like yellow rays. He sat down on the bay side, resting his back on the tabletop, and stretched his arms wide along the top. Anita sat to his left and swung her legs up and across his lap. She then snuggled into him, curling her arms around his neck. Scott kissed the top of her head.

"It's like a piece of your soul has been shredded, and the remnants of your damaged emotions hang like fragile drapes, like in the old abandoned houses on Portsmouth Island. Do you remember how tattered and torn they were?" he asked. "They just hung there stoically for years, constantly blocking out the relentless rays of the sun magnified by the old glass frames."

Anita gently nodded.

"They were so delicate that the slightest tug on the fabric would cause them to fall apart like dust. Same with the memories of war, of killing someone. Your senses become so raw that the slightest hint of that horrible memory singes your nerve endings, threatening to disintegrate your soul. After a while you learn to deal with it, to push it away, but it never really goes away, that threat of annihilation of who you are as a man. You just get good at hiding the outward signs of the raging horror inside you. Most of the time, you're hiding in the shadows, hiding from the memories. It's never a good place and it never ceases to be a part of you." He inhaled deeply, his breath quivering slightly, then exhaled. "That's what it's like."

"My God," Anita whispered. She squeezed him closer to her. "I understand."

Scott paused as he allowed a tear to escape and tumble down his cheek and throat. He sniffed. "Nah, you don't understand, no one does. How can you possibly? I wouldn't want you to. Only those who've experienced it understand, and even then, the reaction is different for each person. A personalized horror story, tailored to each of us who've killed another."

A whippoorwill let out its quick call at the wood line, and Scott stopped speaking long enough to enjoy its serenade. He quietly wiped away his tears.

"Things are going to be a little different now," he said with a hint of anger in his voice, just hidden behind his words. "I will have to talk about this eventually. There's going to be times when I desperately need to speak to someone. I . . . I will need someone to listen to me. Do you understand what I'm trying to say?"

Anita nodded her head again. He could feel it moving on his chest, her hair mussed up against his shirt.

The night had fully arrived, the sky dark above them, tranquil and void of clouds so as not to mask the twinkling stars revealing the full beauty of the Milky Way. Millions of stars in every direction made their way out onto the evening stage, joining the moon to watch over the enchanted sands of the Outer Banks.

CHAPTER TWELVE

August 2006

A few days later, Briggs was on his hands and knees cleaning the interior of his boat.

"How are you, old man?" a voice boomed behind him.

Briggs stood and turned toward the man standing on the dock.

"I'll be damned. Lieutenant Check!" Briggs hopped onto the dock and extended his hand. "What are you doing here?"

"Well, that's a long story, which I'll explain to you when you take me fishing tomorrow."

"You bet. Errr . . . did you get out or something?" Briggs asked, pointing at the moustache on Check's face.

"Or something," Check replied laughing. "I'm still a Marine, just working in a different department. That's why I can get away with the longer hair and a fairly decent moustache. Oh, and I'm a full bird colonel now too."

"That's awesome, sir."

"Listen. I have to be somewhere right now," Check said, looking at his watch, "but let's talk more tomorrow, say around ten?"

"You said you wanted to go fishing?"

"That I do."

"Better make it 0600. The fish bite better at that hour."

Check paused, and Briggs could see he was going through a

checklist of things to do in his head. "You got it, Scott. See you at 0600."

Check waved good-bye and walked back across the yard toward his car. Briggs watched him from the dock, confused. It had been more than a year since they'd last seen each other. Why had Check shown up at his home? Why had Check called him by his first name?

Briggs shrugged and went back to cleaning his boat, but he had a strong sense that Colonel Check hadn't stopped by for a casual visit. Something was up. Great, he thought. I won't sleep a wink wondering what the hell tomorrow is going to bring.

———◆———

The morning sun gently rose over Core Banks—barrier islands that were a part of the Outer Banks—just bright enough to outshine the lighthouse lamp at Cape Lookout. The changing of the guard from the lighthouse lamp to the sun was completed once again as it had been done for over a hundred years. One sentry relieved the other to stand guard over the shimmering sands of the Outer Banks.

Briggs was enjoying the view as Check stomped onto the long pier, carrying a small cooler.

"Right on time," Briggs called out from his boat. "What you got there?" He shielded his eyes from the glare as Check stood at the edge of the pier with the bright morning light behind him.

"Sandwiches and a little liquid motivation."

"I was hoping you would say that." Scott took the cooler from Check and secured it under the seat of his twenty-one-foot Carolina skiff. It was a small center-console, flat-bottom boat capable of navigating the shallow waters behind the banks and marshes—and carrying two former comrades-in-arms for a day of fishing pleasure.

"So where to?" Check settled into his seat.

"You like trout?"

Check nodded with a wide grin. "I was hoping you would say that." Briggs pushed the throttle forward and raced into the rising sun of the new day.

They sat adrift not too far from a shallow marsh and put their lines over the side with live shrimp on short leaders dangling beneath large orange bobbers. They sat in amicable silence for a while.

"Son, a very powerful man is going to contact you shortly." Check broke the silence and looked up from reloading his hook. He had Scott's full attention. "This guy, his name is Shelby Trust. He's a Texas billionaire whose father and grandfather made it big drilling for oil in Texas, Oklahoma, and California."

"Should I know him?"

"Not directly. He's Jeff Blake's uncle."

Scott squinted his eyes, looking out over the waters. Finally, his gaze returned to Check.

"The Trust name is synonymous with power and wealth. They've had their fingers in foreign and offshore markets, and manipulated local governments to take away landowners' rights in order to obtain resources. When the government started looking too closely into the Trust fortune, the family turned their attention to third-world countries with uneducated labor and built a foundation that claimed to help those in need. They were actually taking advantage of people who would work for a basket of food, people who lived in constant fear that thugs would uproot them from their homes if they did not perform for the bosses. They hide behind the Trust Foundation that builds new schools in South America and Africa, but it's a rouse in order to manipulate futures on the world market. Believe me, these are not nice people."

"Okay" was all Brigg's could think to say. He wasn't sure where this was leading.

"Okay then." Check was silent for a few moments then returned his gaze to Briggs. "I now work for a special unit in the military, and we're quite certain that Shelby Trust will contact you, and we want you to go along with his requests, whatever they may be. Most importantly, we want you to give us anything he may give you so we can inspect it. At no time should you act suspicious or question Mr. Trust too much, but you should give off the impression of having a natural curiosity about him. Nothing more. Do you understand what I'm saying?" He raised an eyebrow at Scott.

Briggs touched his fishing line as he tried to gather his thoughts around why Trust would want to contact him and exactly what Check was asking of him. "Are you saying you want me to be a spy?"

Check's expression became even more serious. "Shelby Trust is not only wealthy; he is friendly, likeable even. He will use his manner and his money to win you over, make you feel as if he's taken you under his wing. Don't be fooled by all that. As is typically the case with Trust, his goal is to gain leverage and control over any person or situation to benefit his end goal."

"What exactly does he want from me?"

"I can't go into details. It's just paramount that you play along with whatever game Trust asks you to play. Allow him to manipulate you, so to speak."

Scott winced. He was a man who liked being in control of his own life. Agreeing to be manipulated didn't feel right.

"If Trust has confidence in you, he will make you a part of his network of trusted people," Check added. "And he pays well."

"So how rich is this guy?" Briggs slowly turned the handle on his fishing reel. "And why would he pay me? What will I be expected to do?"

Check drew a long breath and squinted as he faced the sun,

now in full view above Core Banks. "We think his worth is in the fifteen-billion ballpark. As to why he'll pay you—it has to do with some special favors he'll be asking you to do."

"Fifteen-billion ballpark?" Briggs didn't even hear the rest of what Check said as he tried to comprehend that kind of wealth.

"Ballpark. It's hard to tell because of the way he has his assets arranged. But Scott, this is the thing you need to know. Money is not his motivation. It is power and ownership. Money is the means to the end—what he uses to motivate so he can dominate."

"Okay." Brigg's mind buzzed as he tried to make sense of what Check was saying. "You want me to let him lead me, but to stay aware of his ulterior motives. And to share everything with you."

"Right," Check confirmed. "Let him impress you with his wealth. Hell, he'll probably take you fishing."

They both let out a slight laugh, just enough to vent some of the tension that was building as they stepped into a different relationship—that of spy and handler. Briggs gazed out over the beautiful emerald green water that stretched out from the end of the marsh and meandered its way into the sun.

It sure sounded as though Check wanted him to be a spy and maybe eventually a spook, someone who worked on the fringes of the government payroll. A disposable hero, never recognized, always in the shadows, fairly expendable. A whipping boy for the government's secret army who received money from line items on obscure bills passed quietly through Congress.

Briggs set his fishing pole in a rod holder, leaned his elbows on his knees, and looked Check straight in the eye.

"I'm going to take a wild guess here. If I say no, it's all over for me. No more Corps. I don't go back to Iraq and our fishing trip is over. Don't pass go, don't collect two hundred bucks."

Check held his gaze. "Yes, that's pretty much it. Once I initiated this conversation, your future was placed in one of two directions. If you say no, you'll receive an honorable discharge at the rank of staff sergeant, effective immediately. In return for your silence, we keep up your benefits. Your discharge will be based on your medical disabilities due to your past combat wounds. You will live pretty well, as long as you don't speak a word about this conversation to anyone. Ever."

"Or?"

"Or you can say yes and help me catch a very powerful bad guy."

Briggs looked away and chewed his lip, deep in thought.

After a few moments of silence, Check said, "I want to be clear: my job is to catch this guy. This will be a long mission, Briggs. Victory will not happen overnight. I want you to understand that you'll be under for a long time, as it will be completely determined by Shelby Trust's timing. You will be well compensated for your services. I got you cleared up to a GS-10 pay, equivalent to a captain's pay. We'll have to be careful how we get you your paychecks."

Briggs twisted in his seat, feeling trapped by the conversation. He desperately wanted to stand up and walk around so that he could find a space where he could think. He felt as if he were trapped in the van with his family on the way back from boot camp when the topic of Anita was brought up, or beneath the rubble of the building with the dead Jordanian. Shit, he thought, and then with all the talents of an actor, he mustered an expression of total control.

Briggs leaned over the edge of the gunwale and looked out over the short trees and brush clinging to the seemingly endless banks of sand. "This explains the generous amount of leave for my convalescence."

"Yes, it does. We are on Trust's time now, so you stay here until he shows up," Check said matter-of-factly.

"What if he doesn't show?" Briggs asked.

"Oh, he'll show all right, but either way you decide, we are still finishing up our fishing trip. God, this place is beautiful." He turned his face into the slight morning breeze and filled his chest with the salty air.

Briggs chuckled, then did the same. "You know, there was a time when I couldn't wait to get out of this place. All I dreamed of was something better, bigger, something more. I just wanted to get away and find my future . . . away from here."

Check opened the cooler, handed a beer to Scott, and took one for himself. He nodded, but didn't say a word.

Briggs continued. "I was fourteen when my dad died, and I knew I wanted to be a Marine. That was my whole focus and motivation. It was the only reason I graduated high school. I would have just run away and gotten a crummy job, but my recruiter said I couldn't join if I didn't graduate. I even played my hold card by telling him my father had won the Congressional Medal of Honor. Of course, he already knew that. Told me it wouldn't help get me enlisted in boot camp if I didn't have a high school diploma. God, I dreaded school. But I stuck it out. I graduated. You know the rest."

Check nodded again, sipped his beer. Briggs opened his can and took a big gulp. He held it up to the light. "Courage," Briggs said.

Check raised his beer in salute.

Briggs smiled. "After all I have done and seen as a Marine, all I wanted to do was get back to this place and fish. I finally understand the security in my father's dream to live on these waters—the future I had been trying to avoid. And I have found my future, Colonel. It's here, on the leathery backs of the sea turtles that surface next to my boat in the early dawn."

"Eloquent," Check said with a smirk.

Briggs shook his head, smiling. "Yeah, whatever."

"Did your father speak much about the war?" Check asked suddenly.

Briggs took a moment to answer. "No. He never tried to influence me on whether I joined the service or not. It has taken this long for me to realize that he was the happiest and most content when he was here in this wonderful place that he called home, that I call home." Briggs took another gulp of his beer. "So your offer of a fixed retirement is very enticing at this point in my life."

Check peered into the water at the edge of the boat and nodded. "Well, that's good for me too."

"I was looking forward to the end of my enlistment," Briggs continued. "I was even thinking about going to college, so the idea of paid retirement right here and now . . . well, I like the idea, especially as me and my girl just got back together." Briggs spotted several red drum chasing bait in their direction. The opportunity was perfect to hook one of them and seize the catch of the day, but he was distracted by the intensity of the conversation. He looked away from the approaching fish and turned his attention back to Check.

"I'm not entirely sure what I'm saying yes to, but I've gotten used to catching bad guys, so I'll do it."

Check shifted in his seat and flashed a grin of relief.

"You know a lot about me, Colonel. You've seen my files, you knew how to find me. You showed up here unannounced and knew I would welcome you, knew we would fish. You knew I would say yes to this mission. You've fought beside me in battle, as a brother and a Marine. Your face was the first I saw when I woke from hell and realized I wasn't dead. I think you and I share a bond much stronger than blood, and that is why I trust you." Scott paused. "But there is something about me that you will not find mingled in with all the rhetoric and statistics. I am of this place and it is of me. The salt water runs through my veins, and I have rarely spent a night here without sand in the sheets and the sound of the waves kissing the shore."

Check nodded. "You know, when you said, 'I'll do it,' I was going to shake your hand and say you are doing your country a great service, but you and I both know you're doing it because it is the right thing to do. It's like you just said, Briggs. You are doing it for me, your friend, all your friends in uniform, and for yourself. I promise I will look out for you and your family. I won't let you down, because I know you won't let me down." He reached a hand out to Scott. "Now let me shake your hand."

Briggs grabbed his hand and they shook enthusiastically, both smiling.

"Good, let's get some paperwork out of the way." Check removed a small video camera from his bag. He spent the next few minutes recording statements of intent from both he and Briggs as he shook Briggs's hand and formally welcomed him into what he called "The Service." Then he returned the video camera to his bag and handed Briggs a set of discharge papers from the Marine Corps. Then he gave him another that inducted him into The Service.

Check spent several minutes explaining the particulars to Briggs in simple terms. He explained that being a Marine would now simply be Briggs's cover for his existence in The Service, and that his money now came from a different government source and not directly through the Marine Corps. He was going to be in the shadows. The job was renewable on a case-by-case or mission basis. At any time and for any reason, Scott could be retired or moved to another mission. Check explained that one day Scott could be moved to New York to work on the back of a garbage truck, if that was what the job called for. Or he could lie dormant for months, during which time he would train, honing and learning skills for upcoming missions. He stressed that Briggs was in for life once he agreed. Briggs was filled with both apprehension and excitement as he swore that he understood his new role.

Check produced a small stainless steel flask. "Remember I promised that you and I would share a drink of good scotch one day? I think we're ready for that drink now." Check passed the flask to Briggs.

"So this is the good stuff?"

"Only the best. I think it's called for, don't you?"

"Yes, I do." Briggs took a long pull from the flask. He signed the paperwork and the video disk and handed them back to Check.

"So now it's done?" Scott asked. Questions tumbled around in his mind, but he instinctively knew that they wouldn't be answered at this time or in this place.

"Not quite, my friend. We are doing this back-assward because of the constraints of time. We will train you later at the academy. For now, the game is on, so we are playing catch up."

Briggs took another sip from the flask. "This flask is pretty beat up," he said.

"Yes, it is sort of a casualty of war. It's old and beat up, but I like things like that. It's a bit like me."

Briggs laughed.

"Of course, I will replace it when it starts to leak."

Briggs examined one of the corners that looked as if it had been soldered before passing the flask back to Check. "Looks like it did leak."

"Yeah." Check grinned and lifted the flask to his lips. "I meant, when it leaks again."

Briggs turned the boat back in the direction of his dock. They pulled up to the pier, unloaded the boat, and sat down at the picnic table in the backyard. It was still early so they were all alone.

"Now for the cool stuff." Check reached into his pocket and

passed Briggs a small cell phone. "This phone is your direct connection to me and the command operation." Check handed him a sheet of paper. "This is a bit like school, so I apologize in advance, but you have to memorize the phone numbers on that sheet."

Briggs gave an exaggerated eye roll. "The first one is easy."

"How so?" Check enquired.

"It's the day I became a Marine, 6-18-2004."

"How about that. What an odd coincidence." Check flashed a narrow smile.

Briggs nodded, but his mind was turning. *I don't think there are any coincidences in this line of work. He was so sure I would say yes, he set the phone number up ahead of time. A small whisper of suspicion formed in his mind.*

Check continued, "All right now, this phone is a little different than regular phones. Any time you dial a secure number, the phone will automatically erase the number from its memory. That way, if somebody picks it up, they won't be able to trace any of the secure numbers. Other than that, it operates normally. It can only be used after entering this five-digit code." He handed Briggs a piece of paper with the code.

"You got it?"

Briggs nodded.

"Are you sure? Because the numbers are random this time."

Briggs nodded again, and Check folded up the paper and stuck it back in his pocket.

"Aren't you going to break out a lighter and burn that or something?"

"No. Not here." Check's tone was serious. "If an incorrect code is entered five sequential times, the phone will lock up and automatically activate a distress signal that won't be audible to the human ear. A booster tower will pick up and enhance the signal.

You can also activate the emergency locator using another code, which is listed on the first sheet."

"Right." Briggs turned the phone in his palm.

"Oh, and one of the drawbacks to this phone is that the line can be accessed from our end at any time, so that we can listen to ongoing conversations, sometimes without your knowledge."

Briggs made a face.

"So don't take it on any hot dates," Check joked.

"Understood."

Check pulled out a watch from his pocket and dangled it enticingly. "Will anyone notice if you start wearing a new watch?"

"I doubt it. I'm always buying new ones because I beat the hell out of them. Scratched, broken, lost. You name it." He examined the watch in Check's fingertips. It was sturdily built, with a stainless steel case, a thick fabric band, and hands for hours, minutes, and seconds in the center of a slate-gray background. Slightly left of the movement, there was a date counter. The bezel rotated in one direction for diving times, and a small compass was mounted on the band.

"This is another type of locating device," Check explained. He demonstrated by pulling the bezel out and rotating it in a clockwise direction. "Doing this will activate a distress signal."

Check handed the watch to Briggs. "Both the watch and the phone have an ID number in it, which would give pertinent information to ID you when scanned."

"Do I get a cyanide capsule?" Briggs asked jokingly.

Check's expression changed. "No, that's only for people who know something they don't want to reveal during torture. And trust me, if you're tortured properly, you'll tell everything you know."

Briggs saw the stone-cold, somber face before him, and the

gravity of what he had signed up for started to dawn upon him. There was a moment of silence between them.

When Check spoke again, his tone was lighter. "I can't tell you any more about Trust. You will have to feel him out for yourself. I will fill you in as we go along, but I don't want to place any preconceptions about him in your head. You will have less to lie about, less to worry about, and you will appear more natural. Believe me, the guy's not an idiot. He will work you over in a conversation; even in a little chat he will be gathering information, making assessments. He is a naturally suspicious person—has been all his life."

Check slapped his thighs and rose from the bench. "Remember, do not let the phone out of your sight. In particular, don't let it get into the hands of Trust or his people. They may try to trace back the signal with some device, and even though they won't be able to read it, their failure to do so will set him off. He'll run from you like a trophy buck from a noisy hunter.

"Now, when you are using the phone, you can bet he will also try to read your outgoing signal, but don't worry about that." Check held out a small bag that looked like a Ziploc sandwich bag. "This liner should be kept in your pocket. When you're not using the phone, keep it in the liner. Just having this liner in your pocket will scramble the device of anyone trying to eavesdrop electronically on your phone call. The plastic is not really plastic; it's a type of transparent metal poly. Real space-age technology. Even if somebody picks it up and plays around with it, they will never know the difference between this and a sandwich bag. I'll make sure you get a couple more. Oh, and the phone does not ring; it only vibrates. And remember the watch has an emergency alert on it, so don't activate it unless you have to."

"I will just leave it at home," Briggs said.

"No, wear it. Trust will notice the tan lines on your wrist and wonder why you are not wearing a watch."

"Shit." Briggs stood up, massaging his forehead. "You really threw me on top of an alligator. Why me?"

"I can't tell you now, but I will when—"

"When I need to know," Briggs finished.

"This guy is sharp, but you are sharper," Check said, pointing a finger at him. "That's why I am using you."

"But I get a sense that's not the only reason. It sounds crazy, but I think it's also because I'm somehow involved." Briggs held up his hands. "I know, you can't tell me. Just take care of my family if something happens to me."

"That's the deal. You are due to go back to Iraq in twenty-six days as if nothing has changed. Until then, our contact will be through this phone. Give me a call when he tries to contact you, and at least once a day to check in. Doesn't matter what time. And don't tell a soul about any of this."

CHAPTER THIRTEEN

August 2006

The days passed agonizingly slow for Briggs, as if he were digging a hole in the sand that kept filling in. He could not sleep nor get any rest no matter how hard he tried. He was so nervous and distracted that he couldn't fish either, and that was the most frustrating part. Immediately after Check departed, Briggs was overwhelmed by the new twist in his life. He could feel his blood racing at top speed. There was a part of him—a part he never really understood—that craved the kind of excitement and even danger that his new life offered.

Despite his stress, he spent every moment he could with Anita when she wasn't at work, and he had started to spend more time with Sweetie too. He and Anita agreed that a gradual introduction into Sweetie's life would be best. She was as precious as could be, and he loved everything about her without prejudice. He could easily see himself as her father, even though it was a bit of a "cart before the horse" situation. He was certain of one thing—they would be his family.

Of course, since Check's visit, even that simple goal—creating a family with Anita and Sweetie—had gotten more complicated. Still, Scott was determined to find a way.

When he was alone with his thoughts, his mind filled with questions that came at him like machine-gun fire. What have I gotten myself into? Will I be hauled away to meet Trust? Should I carry a weapon? Will I have to kill someone? Is Check using me? Am I an expendable pawn for his greater gain? Should I have just taken the retirement and not accepted Check's challenge?

He would shake his head and breathe deeply, audibly—in and out, in and out. *Lose the doubt, dumbass. Lose it now. Focus. Stay on task.*

He knew he couldn't have any nerves or preconceived notions. Check had emphasized that Trust was sharp and had instincts for bullshit and trouble. Scott had to go in calm and clean.

◆

Two weeks after Check came to see him, Scott was walking down to the dock carrying a can of gas for his morning trip to inspect the flounder net that ran from the end of his pier to the deeper water at the edge of the channel when his "super phone" vibrated. It was probably Check calling—as he had done every morning—to get a status report. Scott pulled it from the plastic baggie in his pocket and answered it.

"Good morning! How's the fishing today?" Check's tone was jovial at first, then grew more serious. "Last night, Trust's men arrived in Morehead City, North Carolina, and checked into a hotel. Trust will not be far behind them. Keep your normal schedule, of course, but be prepared for some form of contact from Trust soon. Did you get the care package I sent you?"

"No, not yet," Briggs said, squinting as he looked over the morning water. A few boats were out. "What's in it?"

"Some instructions, a laptop, and your first month's rent."

"Rent?" Briggs was caught off guard by this last part.

"Yes, that is how you will receive compensation to your pay. It will help maintain your cover on this particular mission and keep you on top of your new pay scale without anyone getting suspicious at your Battalion S1. For anyone who wants to know, you are now the proud owner of three rental homes. The deeds and locations are in the paperwork. A realty company in New Bern manages the homes and the renters for you, and they send you a check every month. The homes will always have occupants and will always be maintained. There's nothing for you to worry about. You just collect the rent checks."

"No kid—" Briggs stopped midsentence. One of the boats he'd noticed just moments ago was clearly heading his way. It was small but fast and coming out of the channel into shallow water toward his flounder nets, which were clearly marked by red and blue foam balls that jostled on the surface.

"Scott? What's going on?"

Check's voice brought him back to the phone call. "Not sure. There's this boat—"

"Where are you? Fill me in now." Check's voice demanded a response.

"Hold on, Colonel. Some clown is about to run through my nets."

Briggs placed the phone against his chest and waved his arm in an attempt to alert the oncoming boat to his nets. The lone operator finally saw the net and pulled back on the throttle, letting the decelerating boat settle into the shallow water.

Briggs shouted to the driver, "It's pretty shallow right there. Trim your motor up as far as it will go and you should make it." The man did as Briggs suggested and maintained a slow approach to the pier.

Briggs returned the phone to his ear. "Everything's fine. Maybe this guy doesn't know the area. Pretty damn fine boat, though." He admired the Shearwater twenty-four-foot blue-on-white vessel with its 250 OptiMax on a shallow water jack. He knew how fast those boats could go—this one could run on twelve inches of water wide open at more than seventy-five miles per hour—and he also knew the price tag. Small boat, big price tag: it probably cost around fifty thousand dollars.

"Don't know him?" Check asked.

"Don't know him."

"Describe him."

Briggs lowered his voice a bit. "Late fifties, a little shorter than me maybe, spotty gray hair, potbelly but not fat."

Check said, "That's our man. You're up, big guy."

The Shearwater was now about ten feet from the dock. Briggs returned his phone to the baggie and placed it in his pants pocket. His heart pounded rapidly as he realized his mission had finally begun. No turning back now.

Just follow his lead.

"That's a neat trick," the man said, pointing at the phone in Briggs's pocket. "I never thought of that." He stood on the bow of his boat to hand Briggs a mooring line.

For a moment, Briggs didn't move.

Relax, dumbass!

"Yup, my old man taught me the baggie trick. Don't even want to think about how many cell phones have been saved in the process." Briggs chuckled lightly, trying to seem relaxed.

"Makes good sense," the man said with a dazzling grin, as he dangled the line for Briggs to grab.

Briggs sat on the edge of the dock to stop the boat's forward movement gently with his feet. The man jumped from the boat and secured his stern line to the dock as Briggs tied up the bow.

"Fine morning out there today. I'm Shelby Trust. Thanks for the help." He extended his hand to Briggs, who shook it with a firm grip.

"No problem. Scott Briggs." Even though his pulse was racing, his voice was calm and friendly. *Just keep breathing. Stay cool.*

"That's good news, Scott Briggs. Now I know I have the right dock and the right person." Trust flashed that gleaming grin again and stood with his hands on his hips, chest out.

"Is that so?" Briggs asked.

"You and I have a mutual friend. Jeff Blake is my nephew."

"I know Jeff, sure," Briggs offered. "He okay?"

Trust waved his hands in the air. "Oh, hell yeah. He's just fine. He has written to me about you and your adventures together. It is truly a pleasure to meet you, Scott."

Briggs was immediately enthralled by Trust, with his Hollywood persona and Texas accent. There was something about Trust that reminded him of John Wayne riding atop a magnificent steed. The wealthy Texan was dressed in top-of-the-line fishing attire. His Rolex Oyster complemented his three-hundred-dollar Costa Del Mar sunglasses to a tee.

Briggs smiled to himself. *Okay, Shelby Trust. I am impressed.* But he started wondering about Jeff Blake's connection to all this. Blake had never mentioned his rich Uncle Shelby, not once. And they'd talked about a lot of family history between them.

Trust pointed again at Brigg's pocket where he'd put his phone. "So I bet you got lots of fishing tricks up your sleeve, eh?" he said, abruptly changing the subject. Briggs noticed that his senses bowed up in response. He was a guy whose gut instincts had saved his life more than once. So when his senses bowed up, he paid attention. There was a lot more going on here than the surface interactions were indicating.

"I guess you learn a few tricks growing up around the water," Briggs replied.

Trust nodded, inhaling the morning air, which was as crisp and clean as they come.

The conversation stalled for a moment, and Briggs wasn't

sure what to do about it, until he realized that any normal person would ask why Trust was there. He would raise suspicions if he didn't ask some questions, so he threw one out there.

"So, Mr. Trust. What brings you here to me this morning, besides a few letters from Jeff Blake? The reason I ask is because someone in my line of work who gets a visit from someone in uniform, or from a stranger from another family, is about to get some really bad news, if you know what I mean."

Trust squinted his eyes at him. For a moment, Briggs thought he might have been too abrupt in his questioning. Then Trust started laughing. Loudly.

"Well, hot damn," he said, clapping his hands together. "You get to the point, doncha, son? And please, call me Shelby." He pointed at Briggs. "I like you. And I'd be wondering the same damn thing. Well, let me fill you in."

They walked down the pier to sit on the very bench where Check and Briggs had sat not too long ago.

"You see, Blake's father Jeff Blake Sr. and I grew up together in Texas. We attended Texas A&M as freshmen. Then Jeff Sr. went to school at Baylor University to become a doctor while I stayed at Texas A&M to finish my degree in engineering."

He paused a moment. "Not my idea, that engineering degree," Trust added. "I wanted to be a florist."

Briggs had been staring at the picnic table as he listened, but he whipped up his head to look at Trust at that odd detail.

"I'm sorry. Did you say . . . ?"

A roar of laughter flew from Trust's chest. "Nah, just seein' if you were listening," he said through a fit of chuckles. "You should have seen your face just then." He started to laugh some more.

Briggs couldn't resist, and he started laughing too. "Okay, you have my attention," he said to his odd new friend and nemesis.

Trust went on to tell Briggs about how his relationship with

Janet, the sister of Blake's dad, grew into a loving relationship. He and Janet were soon married in wealthy Texas fashion, and they settled down on a section of the Trust land, owned by his father Lyndon Trust, just outside Austin.

"But our marriage didn't last—only five years." Trust glanced out at the water, a sad smile on his face. "Janet moved on with her life, and so did I. I set my focus on my father's oil business and learned the trade with heart and soul. Then, when my father died in a freak accident on a drilling site, I took over the reins of the company."

"And how did your company lead you to me?" Briggs asked.

Trust smiled. "You led me to you, Scott Briggs."

CHAPTER FOURTEEN

August 2006

Briggs wasn't sure what his next move should be. They had spent more than an hour talking about everything from the war to fishing. Trust didn't seem to want anything except a casual conversation and the promise of a future fishing trip. Briggs came to the conclusion that Trust was an okay guy, and if he didn't know any better, Briggs would easily take Trust into his confidence.

The wind had started to pick up, and the slight chop on the bay between Gloucester and Harkers Islands had turned into a menacing stack of white caps that would surely keep Trust from going back to Morehead City.

"Looks like it will be a rough ride back to—wherever you're staying." Briggs floundered, barely stopping short of saying "Morehead City." That would definitely set off Trust's warning bells. Even though Check had told him Trust's men were in Morehead City, Trust had not. Briggs was starting to understand the "need to know" clause in his new life. Even though it angered the crap out of him each time Check had said, "I can't tell you. Not yet. You'll have to find out on your own. Need-to-know basis," those limited-knowledge rules really made sense. If he had made the Morehead City slip just now, it could have all been over.

Trust didn't seem to have noticed Briggs's almost-slip. "What I thought I would do is have my driver bring a car here and take me back to Taylor's Creek. I'm staying on my boat, docked by the restaurant there. Maybe you could show me a good fishing spot tomorrow. Here's my calling card." He handed it to Briggs. "My cell phone number is listed there. Call and let me know what would be a good time to go." He pulled out his cell phone, which was vibrating, and answered it. He held up a finger with his free hand and motioned that he was going to take a minute to talk. Briggs looked toward the house to see his mother and sister Michelle approaching.

"Who's your friend, Scott?" his mother asked as Michelle wrapped her arms around him and squeezed.

"How's my favorite brother?" She rocked him back and forth, trying to push him off balance.

"Careful, honey. You'll hurt his arm," his mother said.

"It's okay, Mom. It's not bad. It—"

His mother held up her hand, stopping his words. "I'm tired of you coming home all torn up, son. It's bad enough that you are hurt, but that's all I need to know about it. I'm just thankful you're walking and talking, alive. I didn't let your father tell his stories about his war wounds, and I won't let you tell yours. A mother worries, even more than a wife."

Scott broke away from his sister's embrace and hugged his mother.

"I got you, Mom," he mumbled as his sister joined in the group hug.

"Someone smells like fish, and this time, it's not me," Scott teased Michelle, sniffing the air.

She punched him in the chest. "No kidding. It's only my life."

For Michelle, there was just no escaping the smell of fish; it was in the air, on her clothes, on her skin. It came with the fish house territory.

Scott looked over at Trust, who had moved away from them and was standing on the dock, still talking on the phone. Knowing that his mother and sister would want to interrogate the stranger, he said to his mother, "He's the uncle of one of my Marines, but he is a bit strange. So don't make a big fuss, okay? I will tell you about him later."

"Oh, don't be ridiculous. What's his name?"

"Yeah, Scott, don't be such a stick in the mud. Come on, let's go meet him. He looks kind of cute, Mom." Michelle waggled her eyebrows and grabbed her mother by the arm, pulling her along as she headed in Shelby Trust's direction.

"Oh no, the last thing I need is a man. I'll meet him, but that's it."

"Ladies, I'm not sure—" Scott started to tell them to steer clear, but it was useless. They were halfway down the dock before Scott could stop them. He saw Trust end his call and pocket his phone, ready to greet his public.

They introduced themselves to Trust, extending their special brand of Southern hospitality. Briggs pushed away his concerns, remembering Check's instructions to act normal and relax. And so he did, joining in the camaraderie, just like he would have done with any stranger who had pulled up at his dock.

When his mother heard that her visitor had a driver coming out to pick him up, she insisted there was no need for that. They would be more than happy to drive him back to his boat at Taylor's Creek.

But Trust shook his head. "I'm grateful to you, Alma, but I have this limo service at my beck and call all week. I have a better idea, in fact. You three ride out with me and have dinner in Beaufort, then my driver can bring you home. Whady'all say?" He grinned, pleased at his suggestion.

His mother and Michelle looked at Scott. "Well..." he hesitated.

"Please, everyone come. I insist. There is plenty of room in the limo and I can use the charming company."

His mother smiled and nodded. As the group walked back to the house to wait for the limo, Scott's mother and Michelle chatted amicably with Trust. They took a few minutes to freshen up, and when Michelle's husband Mike arrived after working late at the fish market, Trust invited him to join them.

Before they left the house, Briggs decided to leave his cell phone in his room, stashed away behind some books on the shelf above his headboard.

Briggs's plan was to get to the restaurant, have dinner, and get back before 2100, but he quickly realized there would no chance of that. Trust had poured on the charm to his highly receptive audience the second they had met. From the liquor in the limo to the movie theater on board his "boat"—a hundred-and-forty-foot customized steel-hulled yacht built in Holland—the opulence and grandeur that were Trust were hard to ignore. No one in Briggs's family had ever been exposed to such affluence, and they were immensely enjoying Trust's hospitality. The night ended on the open deck of the fly bridge where Trust hoisted a toast to family and to the Corps.

When the evening ended and they began walking from Trust's yacht toward the limo and their ride home, Trust touched Briggs's arm to stop him.

"I would like to talk to you about a favor I'd like you to do for me, but that can wait until morning. Do you know what the weather is going to be like tomorrow?"

Briggs thought for a moment. "I think it will be okay if we set out early."

"And what is early to you, Scott?"

"Before 0600," Briggs replied with a slight grin, certain that Trust wouldn't be up before ten o'clock.

"Perfect!" Trust bellowed happily. "No matter how late I go

to bed, I am always up around 0500 for coffee. If it is not too inconvenient, could you bring the Shearwater over and meet me here in the morning? You can run that boat, can't you?" Trust asked, now grinning widely.

"Hell, does a frog's ass bump the ground? You bet I can!" Briggs was delighted to get a chance at running such a magnificent machine. "Are the keys in it?"

"I left them on your kitchen table just before we headed out. You'll find tackle for trout, drum, and flounder inside the dry boxes. I have fished these waters before." Trust gave Briggs a firm pat on the shoulder and a wink. Then he handed Briggs five one-hundred-dollar bills and said, "Anything else you can think of that we'll need, including gas and ice, grab it. I bet you can put us on some big ones."

Briggs tried to hand the money back. "Sir, this is way too much money, and besides, nothing will be open until later in the morning. I don't need this." Trust pushed the money away, put his arm around Briggs, and turned to walk him off the yacht.

"Scott, I am not bargaining or bribing when I give someone money. I enjoy spending it and being generous with it, so spend it. And if you can think of anything we need while I'm here, get it for us. I will be in Beaufort for a week or two—we'll need at least that much in gas, don't you think?" He patted Briggs on the shoulder again. Briggs nodded then slid into the limo where his family was already waiting.

On the ride home, his mother, sister, and brother-in-law could not stop raving about Trust's generosity.

"Did you notice that he didn't drink?" his mother said. "Shelby said that he never has more than a small sip or two. I find that a little odd."

"Maybe he is a recovering alcoholic like our neighbor Laura, you know, a recovering twelve-stepper," Michelle replied. "Remember when we caught her drunk in our pool at two thirty in the morning last year? She's been on the wagon ever since."

"I don't think he's a recovering alcoholic," his mother said thoughtfully. "I think he's got so much going on in his head that he can't afford to fog it up with liquor."

Scott knew better. As much as everyone liked Shelby Trust—and he was a charmer, no doubt—Scott could see past it. He was no big drinker for the simple reason that he wanted to stay in control at all times. Booze made you slow, lessened your inhibitions, and loosened the tongue. Leaders could never let their guards down, especially ones who had an ulterior motive, be it of good or foul intent. Even though Scott had been briefed very vaguely about Trust, he just didn't seem like the kind of man who would invest money and time with no prospect of a return. There weren't many men who would.

CHAPTER FIFTEEN

August 2006

The limo returned them to their doorstep at two-thirty in the morning, and his sister and brother-in-law headed back to their home. He was hoping to get home earlier so he could spend time with Anita, but that just didn't happen. Scott retrieved his cell phone from his room and stepped out the back door.

The phone had received one phone call with no caller ID. It had to be Check. Scott started dialing him back as he stepped off the porch, but the phone was already vibrating in his hand. "I need you to stop where you are. Don't bring the phone anywhere near that boat. Put it back in the house," Check said without preamble.

Scott immediately tensed and took a step backward as he scanned the yard. To the left, approximately eighty yards away in the thick brush near the woods, his eye—honed by combat training and experience—caught a movement. Scott slowly slid back into the shadows of the house. His first instinct was to retrieve a weapon from his gun safe and flank whoever it was by going out the side door of his room.

The house sat in the middle of eight acres. The back was four acres from the house to the shallow marsh water. The front had approximately four acres of dense bushes and pine trees that led up to the road. The rock drive was cut through the thick woods to the house, which was surrounded by perfectly maintained grass. The house to the side, just twenty-five yards away with a pool in the backyard, was Michelle and Mike's home. Both houses were flanked by thick bushes full of thorny briers and areas that held marsh water. If someone were out there right now, he wouldn't get out very fast. All of this ran through Scott's brain, an automatic sequence of responses—partly learned, partly instinct—to the threat.

Still holding the phone to his ear, he asked, "Colonel, are you here?" He spoke in a low, quiet voice as he made his way back inside through the sliding glass door.

"Yes," Check responded. "I am here, and there are two more of my guys in the woods to the left and right of the back door."

"I saw the one on the left. Where are you? At the end of the dock?"

"You saw me too?" Check asked.

"Just a guess." Scott's pulse began to calm.

"Leave the phone in the house and meet me at the foot of the dock."

Scott quietly stepped into the house, walked to his room, dropped the phone on his bed, stepped back outside, and walked to the foot of the dock. As he did, he caught sight of the man on the righthand side.

"That's a good way to get shot by my neighbor. You wouldn't be the first dingbatter shot by a hightider," Briggs whispered as he met Check on the dock. Check was dressed in black with an earpiece and radio.

"What in hell's a dingbatter?"

"Never mind," Briggs replied. "What the hell is going on?"

"While you and your family were being wined and dined by Shelby, the shifty bastard had his people wire the phones and install listening devices in your house."

"Damn it, this guy is thorough," Briggs said as he felt the anger building inside him.

"You have no idea. He also has his boat rigged to pick up transmissions from your cell phone. That's why I stopped you before you walked down here with it."

"Oh shit," Briggs barked.

"Oh shit what?" Checked echoed.

"When he first came up this morning, I had the phone on. I was talking to you."

"Did you get on the boat while you were talking to me?"

"No. I was on the dock, but I never got on the boat. I placed the phone back inside the Ziploc bag before I got near his boat."

"You're good then. You would have to be within five feet or so. The transmitter is powered by twelve volts and rigged into the GPS."

Check pulled at Briggs's arm in order to steer him toward the end of the dock, deeper into the darkness. Trust was methodical, and Check seemed determined not to be outmaneuvered.

Check knelt on the dock, indicating Briggs should do the same. "Okay, let's you and I take a quick review," he said in a low, gruff voice. "So far, Trust has been able to clear out your house, bug it, and set you up with a boat that can track your movements and phone calls. Oh, and by the way, he got your car and your mother's car as well."

"Damn it," Briggs seethed. "I should have seen this coming! I don't know what he wants yet, and he's out-slicked me already."

"Yep, he is a real smooth operator."

"What do we do? Rip 'em all out?"

"Nah, that will set him off. What we do is keep playing the game. This is how he operates, and he is the best there is. We know this." Check reached into his pocket and handed him a phone that looked the same as the first phone he had been given. "Here is a phone you can use any time anywhere around him. It's just a regular phone, and he will be able to read it, so be careful what you say. The other phone is the only secure one, but don't use the secure one in your car or your mom's car, as he can hear you now."

"And you knew all this info how?" Briggs questioned.

"We have been and will continue to watch you and your house. Christ, I knew he would do this; it was almost a damn guarantee. I have a crew on Brown's Island with big eyes on your house and another crew you didn't see at the turnoff to your road. Six cameras have been installed throughout your yard so we can survey the grounds."

"When did you do all this?" Briggs asked.

"After Trust's guys moved out. The two boys in the woods will leave with me tonight, but the camera crew will be down the road twenty-four seven. We rented a house at the end of the road. It's number 2107, a two-story brick about a hundred yards up the main road. Ah, hell, you know the area," Check said, waving his hand dismissively in the air.

"Man, this is happening fast," Briggs said, scratching his head. The stress in his voice was evident, and Check frowned.

"How are you holding up with all this?" Check asked.

"Just peachy. I'm learning quickly, that's for sure. Is my family in danger?"

"Negative. And if they were, I would move you and Trust would follow. His interest is in you. That's the only reason he is here. All the devices his men left behind are targeted at you, your room, computer, and car."

"But you mentioned my mom's car?"

"They probably weren't sure what car you're driving. Safe bet is to bug both. It's what I would have done."

"I'm starting to get an idea of this guy now. You know, he was hitting on my mom a little."

"Yeah. Can't say it enough—he's a smooth operator, in all aspects of life." Check chuckled. "That's just him slathering on the charm. Plus, not to be disrespectful, but your mom is not his type. He is a big fan of hookers, high-dollar hookers to the tune of around three, four grand a night. Hit it and quit it, that's his take on the female persuasion."

"Just sex," Briggs echoed.

"Exactly, just sex. Hell, he doesn't have time for romance. He will have a girl flown in when he wants to get a little, and she is out the door when he is done. Don't even have a chance to shower, those girls. Good-bye, get up, and go. Then he goes back to work. That's why he never remarried. A wife doesn't fit into the picture for him. Wives ask too many questions and always want an answer. Hookers just want their money."

Briggs looked over Check's shoulder, keeping an eye on the back of the house. "What's up?" Check asked. "You look a little nervous."

"Really? Because I have my best spy face on right now. You just can't see it because it's dark," Briggs said sarcastically.

Check held up his hands in surrender. "Hey, everything is cool, just relax. This is how Trust is, weird and crafty. And we'll be craftier."

"Yeah, but what you are calling smooth and crafty is straight out of a freaking movie or damn spy novel. This son of a bitch has been in my mother's house, invaded her privacy, and all because of me. I don't take that lightly. Hell, even you've done the same damn thing. This is supposed to be *my* deal, not my family's. I hear what you're saying—I'm the one he's after—but I just wish it didn't have to involve my mother and her space." Briggs rubbed his forehead. "Shit, a few weeks ago, I was just Joe Schmuck Marine. Now you have me and my family tangled up with an eavesdropping pervert on a power trip."

"Look, I know this is tough on you. I have been through it myself. One day, I will tell you that story," Check said.

"I guess I better get used to that." Briggs curled his lips in a frustrated expression.

"Ah. Better to be in the dark on some things. It will save your hide in the end. Trust me, as we go along, the idea will be easier to appreciate. You still in?" Check asked.

"Of course I will finish the job. I'm in. I won't let you down, and I know you won't let me down. Besides, I admit I'm starting to understand why I can't know everything. It's a safety test for me more than anything."

Check nodded. "Just a few things before I go. All the guys here and on Brown's Island are going to leave. We have all the surveillance cameras in and the crew who is monitoring them is up the road, so you're covered. There's another emergency signal you can use when all else fails. Throw a chair through any window in the front of the house."

"Seriously? That's a little dramatic, don't you think?" Briggs scoffed.

"Believe me, if it comes down to it, you'll be glad for it." He slapped Briggs's shoulder and changed the subject. "So how did you like the mega boat?"

"It was the most impressive thing I have ever seen in my life. I now have a picture in my head for the term *filthy stinking rich*."

"Yep, that's what he's all about. I gotta respect the guy a little—" Check stopped midsentence, then continued. "Yeah, I can tell you this. Although he was born into the bulk of his money, he did bust his ass to get what he has today, to maintain it."

"I kinda got the sense that he is a workaholic. Definitely a Type A personality."

"I knew you'd pick it up," Check said, pleased. "The guy never sleeps. Do you remember when he said he gets out of bed at 0500 no matter what was going on the night before? He's serious. Maybe sleeps four hours a night."

A light went on in Briggs's eyes at Check's comment. "How do you know that? I left my phone in the house. Are you listening through my watch somehow?"

"Nope. Even if you did take it with you we couldn't access it. Trust has an array of anti-eavesdropping devices on the yacht that crush even the most sophisticated attempts to penetrate inside the hull and outer bulkheads. They do an incredible job of keeping out our listening devices. That's why he had the thing built out of steel and aluminum in Holland—a very accommodating builder. Nah, I picked up the conversation with a direct device aimed at the two of you while you were chatting on the back of the boat." He grinned mischievously. "Like I said, we've got your back all the time."

Briggs started to grind down on his back teeth. He could see now that his privacy, and his family's, had been completely compromised in this deal. The fun was fast running out of this adventure. The dark concealed his emotions and he kept his mouth shut.

Check went on, "Yep, that little boat of his pisses off a lot of people when he sets up dockside. Phones don't work, Internet goes down, and satellite TVs start flipping out. The tech geeks love him. They get a lot of good business going on the docks to 'fix' all the problems. Trust even fakes his own problems so no one gets suspicious." He laughed, shaking his head. "That guy is smooth, I tell ya."

"He wants me to go fishing with him at 0600 and show him some hot spots." Briggs nodded in the direction of Trust's Shearwater tied up to the dock. "Told me to pick him up in his boat, gave me five hundred bucks for supplies, which of course is completely over the top. Won't take the money back either."

"Yeah, heard that too." Check pulled out a map from the inside of his lightweight camouflaged cape-like jacket. Briggs was certain that it was some type of high-tech gear from Check's incredible inventory of super cool equipment only accessible to the upper echelon of special-ops types. It looked as if it could be quickly pulled up over his head in order to break up the human silhouette, allowing another level of camouflage. Briggs noticed the butt of a Glock pistol and two extra magazines tucked inside a shoulder holster beneath Check's left armpit.

Check shined the blue lens of a flashlight onto the map and pointed. "See this area?"

"I know it."

"Take him there and fish up and down this bank. We will be able to watch and track you without being noticed, and we'll be able to hear without using your phone."

Briggs knew Check and his crew would set up in the Cape Lookout lighthouse, high above the meandering edges of Core Banks and Shackleford Banks. The lighthouse stood more than one hundred sixty-three feet tall and had kept watch over mariners for more than one hundred and forty years. It put a sour taste in Briggs's mouth that the lighthouse, after years of noble service, would now be used for spying purposes—not only on Trust, the supposed bad guy, but also on him.

He remembered as a boy how he would get up early to scope out the nets with his father, sometimes in the chill of winter and sometimes in the light breeze of a hot summer's sunrise. He imagined his father standing in the backyard, still and silent, watching the flash of the turning light from the lighthouse. He would say, "There's our way home, boy." The full emotional impact of those lost moments came rushing in, and he took a few deep breaths. Briggs knew Check didn't see the lighthouse for its beauty and emotional value. It was a strategic vantage point, nothing more. *Guess I can't totally blame him. My memories are my own, but damn. Who is Check more concerned about? Trust or me?*

Briggs suddenly felt a surge of anger. He decided to exercise a little of his own power and regain some control. "That's not a good idea, sir," he said mildly. He turned the map sideways and pointed at a different location far away from the lighthouse. "We will be fishing here."

"That's not good, we can't put eyes on you there, and he will be suspicious of any boats that follow, other than his own, of course. He'll probably have one of his boats shadowing you as well."

Briggs grew more confident as he spoke. "That may be true, sir, but we won't be fishing where you are asking us to. When I first met Trust here at the dock, he said he'd fished here before. That means he knows the best places to fish. He knows it's not the time of year for that area. Everyone knows that, even the dingbatters. Add that to the fact that you have a huge lighthouse right there, hanging over the very area. He'll not only be suspicious, but he'll be pissed off if he realizes what we're doing." Briggs raised an eyebrow. "If you really don't want to raise warning flags, and since you know I am able to handle this job without a constant eye on my ass, I think the mission would be best served by letting me take him where the fish are biting." He paused. "Sir."

Check fell silent and let Briggs's words settle in. He lifted his chin, staring straight at Briggs. "You're right."

"Good." Briggs felt a lot more satisfaction than he probably should at his successful power play. It was hard for him not to smirk, but he didn't dare. "It'll be fine. Just a fishing trip, in my own backyard practically. I'll relay the events as soon as I'm able."

"You're right. This is a better move." Check retrieved a radio from his pocket and ordered his men to bug out. "Call me after your fishing trip and fill me in."

"You bet."

Check turned and flashed a red beam of a flashlight several times toward the bay. A small boat without lights, painted flat black, emerged from the dark of the waters, surprising Briggs. The boat had been waiting several yards off the dock, just out of sight. Two large motors were on the back, also painted flat black, tilted all the way up. The jack plates were maxed out in the up position in order to keep the props from dragging the bottom, which was a mere fourteen inches under the rippling surface. The boat didn't make a sound as the driver maneuvered it with an electric trolling motor mounted on the front of the boat. It snaked over to pick up Check, who made a short hop and landed on the front of the craft with a graceful, silent step.

He looked back at Briggs and said, "Be careful. And one day, you'll have to tell me what the hell a dingbatter is."

The boat silently slid back into the dark. Briggs stood at the end of the dock and watched as it stealthily made its way into the bay. He admitted to himself that he was impressed with Check's toys and exit, but he was still pissed off about his family's loss of privacy. He hadn't signed up for that. *I thought I was the spy! Now I'm just getting spied on!* He shook his head. *Maybe the morning will hold some answers,* he thought as he walked back to the house and into his room.

Scott's phone started to vibrate the second he picked it up off the bed. The number was Anita's.

"You're up late," he said while walking toward the back window that overlooked the bay.

"I just wanted to say good night. And tell you I love you." Her voice was soft and sweet—so Anita.

"Now how did you know I would be up this late?" Briggs asked.

"Scott, this is Gloucester, everybody knows everybody. Everyone knows everything." She laughed.

How true. And here I was upset about Check spying on me. He laughed. "You have no idea," he said.

"What?"

"Never mind. I'm sorry we were out so late. I tried to get back earlier but there was no escape. The visit lasted longer than I thought it would."

"I understand. Anyway, I get off work tomorrow . . ." She paused. "I mean today, at three in the afternoon. Wanna get together after that?"

Briggs smiled. "Nothing, I mean nothing, would be better. I'll pick you up."

He looked out the window toward the water as they said their good-byes. The only indication that a boat was on the water was the white foam spraying up behind it as it passed in front of the shimmering moonlight dancing across the bay.

CHAPTER SIXTEEN

August 2006

Briggs's bleary eyes bulged when he saw that it was seven o'clock. He'd slept maybe two hours, and even those were unsatisfying. At one point, he'd thought about going out for a run and perhaps coaxing Anita out of her house for some moonlight romance down by the water's edge. Just the thought of a clandestine meeting with her had excited him to the point of arousal until he thought about Check's men following him, watching and listening. *Damn, this is going to be a helluva wet blanket on my love life.*

The morning light brought no answers to the questions that kept Briggs restless in his bed throughout the night. He wondered about these new chains that bound him. From now on, every word he spoke with Anita would be filtered because he knew they were being listened to. No more long, honest talks like they used to have. It killed a part of him just thinking that he could not be himself with her. But it was for her own safety. And his mom. His sister. His friends. The reality of the constant surveillance they were under was overwhelming. He was living in a fishbowl with no drapes. "Sucks," he admitted to the walls of his room in a low voice, because he remembered the walls had ears too. His confessionals would have to stay within the confines of his mind.

He thought about the phone and watch that Check had given him and pondered what other gear Check and the Service used that he didn't even know about. His paranoia rose with every thought. In the days since Check had first come to see him, Briggs had already changed some of the habits that had been with him all his life. He no longer slept in the nude; instead, he wore running shorts. He moved his Beretta 9mm from the gun safe and kept it behind a stack of Tom Clancy novels on the shelf above his headboard. He even closed the door to his bathroom in his room, something he had never done before.

Glancing at the clock once more, he shot out of bed and rushed around his room, bouncing off the walls as he dressed to go fishing.

"Shit, shit, shit!" he barked as he banged his still tender arm into the bathroom wall.

"Are you okay?" His mother—always been an early riser—pushed open the door to his room.

"Yes, I just bumped my arm on the doorjamb."

"Your arm? You mean the arm that doesn't hurt at all? The one you said was fine and doesn't hurt?"

"Yes, Mom, that arm," Scott replied, knowing that he couldn't get anything past his mom.

"Can I fix you something to eat for breakfast?" She held a steaming cup of coffee to her lips and Scott's mouth watered. Coffee would be so good.

"No thanks, I'm running late. I should've already been on the water and on my way to Mr. Trust's boat."

"I heard you tossing about last night. Only natural you'd need to sleep in. Who was that man you were speaking to at the end of the dock?"

Scott froze but recovered quickly. "You know what, Mom? I would love a breakfast sandwich. Can you throw a few together for me and Mr. Trust?"

"Sure, honey. I know you're in a hurry. It will only take a few minutes."

"Thank you, God," he mouthed to the heavens. His mother had superpowers when it came to the goings-on around the house. He'd always been convinced she could hear through ten-foot-thick concrete walls. He laughed to himself. Check could train under his mother. At least he'd avoided her question for the moment and given himself a few minutes to come up with an excuse.

Now, not only would he have to watch what he said, but he would have to keep up with everyone else as well. A flash of panic caused him to flush with sweat. The situation was quickly becoming a big damn mountain of hell. All of Check's men had been well armed last night, and Check carried a Glock with two magazines. Scott knew a firefight could get out of hand quickly, and automatic weapons fire—no matter how good a shooter—would indiscriminately bounce off walls and choose its own target.

His mind continued to race. His heart was keeping pace.

Scott walked into the kitchen and helped his mom pack the sandwiches.

"The guy on the dock last night was gigging flounder in the shallows," he said offhandedly, praying that would satisfy her curiosity.

"Really?" she said. "I didn't see any floodlights on the boat."

"They had problems with their lights and were trying to get them to work when I stumbled on him. I thought they were trying to steal Mr. Trust's boat until I started talking to the guy."

Briggs hoped that was the end of the conversation and mercifully it was.

"Well, here you go, sweetie. Have fun, and I'll see you when you get back. Do you know what time?" She gave him a hug and followed him to the door.

"I have no idea, but I will call you and let you know if I can."

The door closed behind him. Briggs was already exhausted from fighting back the fear of exposure. He was quickly walking toward the dock when his mother's voice came at him, piercing and excited.

"Scott! Wait!"

His panic meter moved a level higher and almost made him sick to his stomach. He turned to see her holding out a set of keys. The keys to the Shearwater.

"You'll need these, eh?" She winked and seized the opportunity to kiss him on the forehead. "Are you feeling well? You're a little sweaty."

"No, I'm fine. I'm just in a hurry."

For what, he just wished he knew.

◆

The power of the Shearwater was amazing and addictive. Briggs had never in his life captained such a machine, even though he'd spent the majority of his life on the water—in boats or falling out of them. The throttle begged for the caress of his hand and teased him to push it as far as it would go. The speedometer read fifty-eight miles per hour at only half throttle, its hull barely touching the water. The paddle controls mounted on the steering wheel allowed him to trim the jack plate and the motor without removing his hands from the wheel. It was a good thing too, because just glancing down at the gauges was a distraction that could cause him to lose control of the incredibly fast boat. He flexed his left index finger and adjusted the trim tabs, then used his right index finger to lift the jack plate, allowing the motor to rise and the hull to plane even higher out of the water.

The wind blasted at his face and the water whistled beneath the long lines of the lower hull. Once he got the hang of the controls, he felt confident enough to max out the throttle. A push of his right hand instantaneously launched the boat to seventy-eight miles per hour as the powerful Mercury outboard motor roared to life. *Talk about power. Damn!* It was all he could do just to hang on to the steering wheel while he firewalled the throttle.

He let out a scream of elation, not caring if he could be heard. All the anxiety and pressure that was knotted up inside him was being released to the wind behind him. Gone. For now.

The rush was intense, similar to the adrenaline that would course through his veins during combat, only this time without bullets flying in his direction. In combat, staring into the face of death and winning, the electric charge of being in control of something so deadly and dangerous, was exhilarating. Now, with the power of this magnificent boat in his hands, he wanted to push it to the max. He wanted to stretch out as far on the edge of it as he could, on the very edge of control.

Briggs arrived at Trust's yacht a little late. He waved as he approached, still tweaked from the exhilaration of the ride.

"Sorry I'm late," Briggs said as he eased the Shearwater up to the back of the massive yacht. Trust smiled as he placed his foot on the gunnels of the boat in order to bring it to a total stop before he stepped into the bottom of it.

When Trust was in the boat, Briggs pointed in the direction of one of the seats. "I brought a thermos full of coffee and a bag of sandwiches. There's plenty for you too."

Briggs then put the boat in reverse to slide away from the stern of the yacht. There was a slight hint of fog hanging just on top of the water with no wind to hasten it away. Briggs stayed focused on that and it kept him calm. He was sure he would feel nervous or at least pissed off because of what Trust had done to his house. *I should take you out into the Atlantic as far as I can go and shove your ass overboard*, he thought. Then Trust started up the first of many conversations, and his tone was soft and quiet, respectful of the awakening morning, and Briggs settled into the comfort of the moment.

Trust and Briggs fit together in the boat. Never got in each other's way, never crossed the line, and only spoke in terms of excitement when one of them hooked a fish. It was exactly how it was when he fished with his father. They were like two professionals conducting business on such a level that there was no need for the clutter of irrelevant chatter. Briggs was surprised that he was starting to like Trust, but the distrust was ever present, hanging like the fog around them. This man had bugged his house and invaded his privacy, and more importantly, the privacy of his family who was not involved in any way.

They spent the entire morning fishing from one spot to the next between Morehead and Beaufort. They even managed to hit a few spots by Shackleford Banks, and Briggs made sure they were clear of the lighthouse at all times. Briggs didn't like being under constant surveillance by Check. Either he trusted him or he didn't. If Check was going to spy on him, Briggs was going to make sure he'd have to work for it—hard.

They stopped fishing around noon and drove back to the yacht for lunch. Trust informed Briggs he had organized a feast for them on the top deck. As they approached, a beautiful girl appeared and called for the bowline of the Shearwater. Trust tossed it to her. Standing on the dock, she smiled, caught the line, and tied it up. She was remarkably attractive, standing about five-foot-three, with short brown hair and glistening, tanned skin. Barefoot, she wore white shorts and a light blue T-shirt with a picture of the yacht on it, and its name, Sereniteit—Dutch for serenity—with a setting sun in the background. A hooker? Briggs couldn't be sure. She didn't seem like one, but it was more likely than not, he supposed.

She hugged Trust as he stepped off the Shearwater and onto the dock. "Did you have fun, Uncle Shelby?"

Wrong-o.

Trust hugged the girl and turned her to meet Briggs. "Scott, meet Jenny, the daughter of my captain, David Haynes."

"Happy to meet you," Jenny politely smiled in his direction.

Briggs felt his face flush when he touched her hand.

Trust said proudly to Jenny, "Scott served in Iraq with my nephew Jeff. And Jenny, let's see," Trust placed his arm across her shoulders and started walking down the dock, "your father and mother have worked for me twenty-one years, and you were born a year after they started, so that makes you twenty. Am I right?"

"Yes, Uncle Shelby, and I know what you are getting at, so don't try to be so coy."

"Coy?" he replied.

"I know all about the party." She winked and started walking up the stairs to the big yacht, stopping on the third step to abruptly look over her shoulder. Briggs flinched—caught—because he was staring at her ass so intently he might have set her shorts on fire. Surely she caught him. He grimaced.

"It's a small boat you know," she said just before she sprinted up the last few steps.

Whether or not Trust noticed Briggs's discomfort, he didn't let on.

"That's one smart kid," he said. "She is headed back to Texas for her junior year at Baylor University. She stays on the boat whenever she can. I adore her and enjoy having her around. But as smart as she is, she does not know—I don't care what she thinks she knows—that I have a brand new BMW waiting for her in Texas." Trust chuckled. "It really is hard to pull anything over on her, so I've got it all set up to be sprung on her back in Texas."

They continued up to the aft promenade deck, where lunch was waiting on the table.

"Did you like the dinner last night?" Trust asked Briggs.

"It was extremely good."

"Good. Then you'll really like lunch. It was prepared by Jenny's mom, Samantha. As you have witnessed, she is an incredible chef. She is also responsible for this." Trust slapped his belly with both hands, laughing.

After lunch, Briggs handed Trust the keys to the Shearwater, expecting that Trust would have the limo take him home. Trust put the keys back in Briggs's hand.

"It's yours to use while you're on leave. Enjoy it."

It was only as he walked back to the boat that Briggs realized that Trust had not mentioned the favor he supposedly wanted to ask.

Briggs pulled the Shearwater up onto a sand bar on Shackleford Banks and walked several yards away from it, just in case. He knew he had to move with sober precaution at every moment. He pulled the new phone out of its protective Ziploc and called in.

"So how did it go today?" Check asked.

"It went well." Briggs's reply was short and curt.

"That's it? You sound a little down. What's up?"

"Hell no, I'm fine," he said, knowing his frustration was showing. "The day with Trust was actually pretty great." Again, he did not elaborate.

After the day he'd spent with Trust, Briggs had questions about Check and what this whole mission was really about. Trust still hadn't asked him for anything, including this favor that Check had talked about. The whole day he and Trust had only spoken about fishing and family. While Briggs was on the yacht, he never saw a hint of weaponry of a military type. He thought he would at least have a sense that something was awry, but he'd felt nothing but relaxed and happy the whole day. Things just weren't stacking up the way Check had said they would. In fact, to the best of his knowledge, the only goons with guns were Check and his men.

Briggs had to say something so Check wouldn't sense the suspicion and doubts that were creeping into his mind. "I basically got out-fished by the guy in my own water. That's hard on a hightider. It cut into my ego deep. He never snagged a hook, lost a hook, nothing. He even caught the first fish, the biggest fish, and the last fish. Helluva fisherman. Didn't see that one coming." Briggs ran his fingers through his hair. "That's really about all there was to it."

Briggs left out a few details on purpose. *We'll see how closely I'm being checked by Check.*

Check gave him kudos for playing it cool and building confidence with Shelby Trust, and the two ended their call.

Scott pulled up to Anita's dock in the Shearwater a little after four o'clock. Sweetie was spending the weekend with her father in Morehead, so the two of them slipped away for a private afternoon on Cape Lookout. They stayed until almost dark, lying on beach towels and talking about their lives as they always had. Briggs felt that their time together was growing short. In less than a week, he would be returning to Iraq with the Marine Corps. It seemed liked there was so much to say and not enough time—ever.

"I know this is a silly question, but are you going to be okay while I'm gone?" Briggs asked, lying on his back with his hands behind his head.

"Yes, I'm going to be better than all right. I have a lot of people looking out for me. It's you that I worry about."

She stood up, shook the sand out of her bikini bottom, and tossed her head to one side, sweeping her long, blonde hair behind her shoulder. Briggs stared at her, entranced. She was stunning and incredibly shapely. If anything, her being a mom had enhanced her sensuality. She was more beautiful than ever. She had always turned heads, but now she possessed an incomparable look of maturity. For as long as he had known her, men would try to flirt with her. She always ignored them, fiercely loyal to him, but she was never rude, except when she was pushed too far by someone's unwanted advances and would flash them a look that would explode granite. A class act in every way.

She dropped down in the sand next to him, landing on her knees. Her full, firm breasts bounced, almost popping out of her bikini top. She leaned into him and kissed him full on the lips.

"That's not fair," Scott mumbled out of the side of his mouth as he continued to kiss her back.

"What's not fair?" she asked.

"Jiggling the girls in the face of a defenseless man."

She laughed, a magical sound, and pulled him to his feet. "Come on, my big, strong Marine. It's time to head home. I'm getting hungry. "

He dropped her off at her dock and ran the boat back to his house so he could get cleaned up for dinner. He took the long way back to his dock because he couldn't resist the urge to scratch the itch of danger. The Shearwater clung to the top of the shallow water like skin stretched across a tight muscle. He pushed the powerful vessel to maximum throttle and skipped it across the water. The slight chop on the bay added to the euphoria and enhanced the danger, occasionally launching the boat two feet in the air. It leaped long, straight lines for thirty feet or so, warning of its flight by the sound of the over-revved engine. Scott was so quick on the throttle that the boat slid back into the water like a long, razor-sharp knife, barely making a splash or a sound. He possessed incredible reflexes that served him well both in combat and in dangerous play.

For the next few days, Trust's boat became his release from the pressures that were quickly building upon him, around him, and in him. Between his situation with Check and Trust and the urge to break his personal vow of celibacy, he would have gone nuts if not for the boat. He was sure of it. Scott's nerves were jumpy.

Check called him after dinner, and Briggs excused himself from the couch where he and Anita were watching TV. His mother was out for the evening, and they had the house to themselves. They'd been lounging comfortably in each other's arms, wrapped in a large blanket with their feet on the coffee table.

"Can I call you back later?" Briggs asked as he walked into his bedroom.

"All okay?"

"You bet." Briggs wondered if he already knew that.

"Okay then. Just check in tomorrow at noon unless you need me sooner for some reason."

Briggs closed the phone and tossed it on his bed.

"Who was that?" Anita asked. She was standing in the doorway, blanket wrapped around her.

He imagined she had nothing on underneath it. Immediately, he was aroused. "Uh, that was the duty check-in on the base. I forgot to call and let them know I am alive, so my buddy covered for me."

Another lie, first of many to come, he thought morosely. Anita lay down on the bed and he settled in beside her. They fell asleep in each other's arms. When they awoke, it was two o'clock.

"I need to be at work in the morning," Anita grumbled sleepily.

They gathered her things, and he walked her to her car and kissed her good-bye.

As her car's lights swept across the wooded area in front of the house, Scott caught the hint of a reflection just inside the wood line. He maintained a poker face, watched until Anita was out of sight, then turned and walked back into the house. When the door shut, he sprinted through the house and out the back door. If there was someone at the wood line wearing night-vision goggles, they would be night blind for about ten minutes after being hit by Anita's headlights. That would allow Briggs plenty of time to get to the far side of the property and slide into the woods behind the bastard.

Briggs crept along the area where he saw the reflection, moving so slowly his shadow cast by the moonlight flowed like silk floating on water. It took him about fifteen minutes to close in on the location at the base of a large privet bush, but he was too late.

All he found was a can of brown spray paint.

He stared at it for a long time before throwing it toward the house, his curses of frustration filling the air.

Defeated, he hung his head and drooped his shoulders like a giant sunflower lost without the sun. He kicked the spray can toward the recycle bin, again and again, until it was close enough for him to pick it up and toss it in.

"I'm headed straight for the nut bin," he said as he returned to the house.

The following day, Briggs called Check to report in, and to his surprise, Check told him that for the time being, he only needed to call if he had something significant to report. Briggs figured that meant one of two things: either Check was backing off to relieve some of the pressure, or Check had so much surveillance on him now that he didn't need to talk to him every day. Either way, Briggs was learning the game as he went along.

After his mother had left later that morning, Briggs searched the house for the devices that had supposedly been planted. He found nothing, though he wasn't sure what he was looking for. Still, a wire was a wire. He peered into the internal workings of his computer, his television set, AC vents, lamps, anywhere that might hold a surveillance device or microphone. Not finding anything was worse than finding something, he determined. He was out of his element at this point, and he felt helpless. He sat on the corner of his bed and stared out the window. He took a long breath and released it, slow and ragged, and then stiffened with a realization.

Maybe they've hidden cameras in the trees!

He knew any cameras would be facing the house, so he walked up the beach along the wood line and cut back into the far side of the woods. Looking high up in the trees, he had fairly quick success finding the first camera. After that, finding the others was easy. He looked for the marks on the pine trees from climbing spikes. Then he climbed the various trees, examined the cameras, careful not to be seen on the business end of the cameras.

Now that he knew what he was looking for, he felt back in control, empowered. Questions lingered in his mind: Who did these cameras belong to? Check or Trust? Some other player in this game he did not know about yet? He was impressed at how cleverly the devices had been set. There were no footprints on the ground, no broken limbs on the trees. They even used spray paint on the trees so the spike marks would not be easily recognized—except they had been. That was where the brown spray paint can had come in; someone had made a careless mistake and left it there.

He returned to the house the same way he came, but carefully, much more carefully. He might have missed a camera.

His phone rang as he stepped through the back door.

It was Trust.

Briggs's pulse shot up like a rocket launched into the air. Busted, he thought, his heart racing. Calm down. It's just a coincidence, you jumpy freak, he chided himself. He was so amped up that he decided to just let the call go to voicemail. He would wait for the message and then listen to it, giving himself more time to cool out. He was a terrible liar. He didn't want to go there if he didn't have to.

Combat is much easier than this.

The message was polite and cordial. Trust wanted to send over a limo and bring everybody over to the yacht for dinner. Briggs called him back and accepted the invite, one of several he would accept from Shelby Trust during what was left of his time at home.

He was beginning to really like the guy. What was there not to like? He was polite, generous, and easy to talk with. If he really was the underhanded, manipulative bad guy Check had described, Trust was hiding it well. Crazy thoughts were crashing around inside his head bouncing from ear to ear as Scott tried to arrange everything so it would make sense. Most of the questions he had now were pointed in Check's direction. All the information he had about Trust came from two sources: his own eyes and experiences with Trust, and from Check. The shadows were growing deeper and darker in his mind. Who should he really trust? For the first time he began to feel that he was being manipulated. So, he made a promise to himself that he would start to exercise some control.

Why not? He thought to himself. *For reasons unknown to me and for reasons held back purposely, they both seem to need me, so that gives me power.*

CHAPTER SEVENTEEN

September 2006

After over a week of early mornings, fishing, and meals on Trust's yacht, along with limo outings and dinners with Scott's entire family, including Anita and Sweetie, Scott and Shelby Trust had become close. Trust had openly admitted his growing fondness for Scott and how he looked forward to spending more time with him and his nephew Jeff Blake when they safely returned home from Iraq. A bond had formed between the two men on the North Carolina coast. Trust had said that being there made him feel like he was home with his own family and friends—something he hadn't felt in a long time.

The day of Scott's return to Iraq arrived much faster than he'd anticipated, and he faced it with all the emotional strength he could muster. His reunion with Anita had infused him with a renewed hope for his future, but it was now intertwined with his obligation to his new life, to Check, the Service, and the mission. There were plenty of positive sides to this obligation. It meant more money for his family—a family he hoped would expand in the future, with Anita at his side. The work also offered him the kind of adrenalin and excitement he thrived on. He knew he would need to find a way to balance these two important parts of his life, which were incredibly different—work and home. Overall, he was happy to have more control over his life and future.

Or so he thought.

When it was time for Scott to head to the airport, he and his family loaded into Trust's limousine for the drive. Trust stayed behind, telling Scott that it was an occasion that should be shared with just his loved ones.

After helping Scott's mother into the limo, Trust handed Scott two boxes.

"These are phones that will work in Iraq," he said with a smile. "I took the liberty to preprogram yours with my numbers. You may use it all you wish, and the bill is on me. The other one is for my nephew."

"This is really generous of you, Trust. I don't know what to say." Briggs looked into Trust's eyes. Although Trust was still smiling, he was wiping away tears.

"Oh, there is a catch. You have to call your mom every week and tell her you are okay, and of course, Anita, too." Trust laughed and shook hands with Briggs, then pulled him to his chest for a hug.

"You got it," Briggs replied, smiling. He studied Trust with a new curiosity as he turned to enter the waiting limo. He pushed his way into the crowded Cadillac and pulled the door shut. Trust gave Briggs a final wave behind the black glass.

Now what the hell am I supposed to think about that? No one is that good of an actor. Briggs frowned, confused by the show of affection. Trust seemed genuinely upset that Briggs was headed back to Iraq. He made a mental note to run it all by Check. *I know Check better than this guy,* he rationalized. *Check and I have real history.*

These were his final thoughts as the limo headed down the long, oyster-shell drive, taking them to Cherry Point Marine Air Base—and Briggs back to hell.

The limo was filled with Scott's family, all wearing happy faces that were masking thoughts of dread. Anita sat close to her man and rested her head on his shoulder, occasionally squeezing his hand. His mother and sister were engaged in a lighthearted conversation about hijacking the limo and going to Las Vegas.

"Seriously, Mr. Trust has okayed it. But we have to return home first in order to pack," they joked with the driver.

"Ladies, you are going to get the driver in trouble, though apparently you two do need a vacation. I think you have been cleaning too many fish," Michelle's husband Mike laughed.

The banter softened the uncomfortable truth: Scott had been wounded twice now and the odds continued to stack against him with every call to duty. His platoon was always at the forefront of major actions and assaults against insurgents, putting him in harm's way far more often. Scott had promised his family this would be his last enlistment. Little did they know that he had signed up for a long-term mission that was racked with its own danger.

He knew everyone would be holding their collective breaths until he was home again, including himself. For now, they'd arrived at the base's main gate.

They exited the limo and he gave his mother, sister, and brother-in-law one last hug and kiss before he made his way over to Anita. She could not hold back her tears as she embraced Scott and whispered in his ear that she loved him—always had, always would. He looked into her soft, brown eyes and gently wiped away her tears as he held her face in his trembling hands. He gave her a last tender kiss. "I love you too. Take care of Sweetie. I will see you in six months."

Then he turned and presented his ID to the Marine Guard at the entrance of the airfield gate. Carrying only two small bags and the two boxes, he walked through the chain-link fence toward the waiting Air Force C-5 Galaxy.

He turned to wave good-bye before boarding the aircraft. It

was an act he had performed many times in the past, and it always played out the same. He would catch the eye of his mother, give her one last wave, and then they would go their separate ways. The only difference this time was that Anita was there, giving the process new meaning. A knot formed in his stomach, a lump in his throat. The next breath Briggs took was a difficult one. Although he was over a hundred yards away, he could still see the worry on Anita's face. The effect on him was profound. *She is the reason my heart beats and the sun rises.* He choked back his emotions and cleared his throat as he waved and turned to grasp the ladder well of the massive C-5.

As he entered the aircraft, he noticed supplies covered in cargo nets and strapped to the floor. There were thousands of boxes of every shape and size, labeled with addresses and codes, each on its way to a specific place for a specific purpose. All of them, right down to the last letter of the smallest word, typed on a single slip of paper, tucked away in the tiniest space, had a purpose. It all had meaning and would in one way or another aid in fighting a war that had gone on far too long.

Looking at the vast amounts of cargo made Briggs feel small and insignificant as he made his way between the bulkhead and the cargo nets in order to reach the seating area in the tail section. As he lumbered through the massive cargo hold of the aircraft, Briggs wondered if what he was doing with Check could actually help end this disdainful war.

Entering the passenger bay in the tail section, he was met by Check, who put his index finger to his lips as he took the two packages from Briggs's hands. He passed them off to a man who took them away to the back of the seating area.

Waiting just long enough for his man to disappear, Check asked, "Is that everything he gave you?"

"Yes," Briggs said. There were six other men on the plane,

all clean cut, tall, and obviously some type of government-issue thugs. They were standing in the far back section of the aircraft, softly talking among themselves.

"What's the big deal about the phone? Does it have some type of listening or tracking device on it?"

"It is much more than that. If it is what we think it is, we have never seen one before. This is the first one to hit the streets, and you are the lucky recipient. This is what the government weapons-systems research team was working on, but we couldn't make it small enough to be practical for combat use. The phone is a communications device that also can send back real-time video, sound, GPS, and two-way communication through a simple earpiece. It works off GPS satellites. The battery is one of the components that we couldn't get right. The battery that Trust came up with is rumored to last for over forty hours before it has to be recharged. He is way ahead of us on that.

"One camera can be clipped to the back of the helmet and another on the front. It has an antenna array that ties into the helmet and connects to a satellite. One of the drawbacks is that it needs several satellites in order to work well; otherwise, it is just another shitty two-way radio. The upside is that when you have the earpiece in, you are connected to an operator. The camera viewers are monitored by the operator; he has three video screens at his command: your forward camera, your rear camera, and the sat cam. He can relay info to you via this phone, providing pretty much all you need to know in order to make a decision that may save your life and change the battlefield.

"It also has a sound-suppression system in it. When both earpieces are in, you can hear everything at normal levels; however, if say a rifle or grenade goes off, it suppresses that sound, even if the flash suppressor of the rifle is right next to your head. You can also jump up the gain in order to hear soft or far-off sounds. You just orient your head in the direction of the sound and ask the operator to boost it up. There are two sound pickups—one on the phone itself, and the other in the earpiece. That makes it hands-free. It picks up vibrations from your inner ear when you wear it."

The man who had taken the boxes reappeared and placed one of the phones and the earpiece in Check's hands. Check held up the molded piece that would fit snugly in the ear and showed Briggs the soft, rubber filler, designed to fit firmly inside the ear without allowing dirt or sound to penetrate the ear canal. "It also picks up your heart rate, so if you're not sure if you're dead, just ask the operator." He snickered, and Briggs grinned.

There have been times when I wasn't sure, Briggs thought.

"Think of this as flawless command and control communication, no matter how spread out your men get. You can be seen at all times on camera, and help is just a few words away. No more yelling across the battlefield or over the sounds of battle. Any questions you have can be answered immediately, smoothing out any concerns about orders or what is happening around you."

Check sat back in his chair, satisfied with his explanation. Briggs reached out and picked up the devices.

"It sounds like the company commanders and lowly lieutenants have found a new way to stay in clean uniforms and sip coffee while guys like me dodge bullets and nurse boot blisters that won't go away," Briggs said solemnly. "So why don't we have something like this? It seems like a good system."

"Well, it is a good system, and we do have something like it, but our system is nowhere near as good."

Briggs handed the phone and earpiece back to Check. "I think it's time you came clean about a few things, Colonel. I am at a point where I need information. What is Shelby up to?"

Check rubbed the stubble on his chin. "You're right. It is time I moved you up to the next level. It's obvious that you've acquired

Trust's confidence. Let's talk about some things." He held up the device close to the overhead lamp so Briggs could have a better look.

"This right here has a lot to do with what is going on, but it's not the whole picture," Check said. "Oil has never been Trust's passion, but it has provided the funds for Trust to do whatever he wanted. And when his father died, one of Trust's first moves was to buy a struggling newspaper in Austin. In less than a decade under Trust's command, the paper became a news monster with its own satellites and plans for more reach. It is now an enormous broadcasting network worth more than the oil side of Trust Industries. More importantly, Trust now controls information and every syllable of every word is for sale.

"But," Check paused, "Trust needs more satellites in the right position in order to make this thing work at its full potential. Right now, Congress will not let him have that. The weapons program is a very competitive market, and the people who are in with high-ranking individuals in Congress get first dibs—and they also get favors. Trust had an 'in' with the research boys, but he screwed it up a few years back and pissed off a lot of people, so his device never got past even the consideration phase. You know, 'the fat kid didn't get picked for the team' sort of thing. So Trust tried blackmailing several congressmen and high-ranking military types."

"Blackmail them with what?" Briggs asked.

"He offered them trips on his private jet to islands off the California and Mexican coast, taking them to secure facilities to view his top-secret labs, but there were also other facilities there, if you know what I mean. Some of the officials who spent the night on the islands indulged in extracurricular activities. Those who did were subjects of many videos and still shots taken from Trust's own satellites."

"What, of them having sex on one of his boats—or in their rooms—something like that?" Briggs asked.

"Oh no, he was slicker than that. Those who played with the—let us say 'the help'—were spooked about being around any building or facility, so the girls led them out into the fields and jungles or onto the long stretches of beach where they all felt safe. There, they would engage in some type of deviant act. Trust played this game for almost a year with several of the upper-ranking types, fishing on offshore boats, late-night parties on Tiki-torch lit balconies and porches. The whole time, Trust was gathering pictures of the action from his operational satellites.

"He then compiled the entire saga into one video file, which was oriented from the operator's position. Each of the girls had Trust's devices hidden on them. In one corner of the video you could see the girl's camera-angle head view, in the other her camera tail view, and in the bottom corner, you could see the overhead shot from the satellite. And of course, the audio.

"It was like high-tech porn. Even the smarter groups who didn't get involved with any bad business, who only went fishing, were the subjects of videos of them fishing. But the girls were on the boat, and the crew had the devices as well, so when Trust made his videos of these trips, he got a double bonus. Each fishing trip was taken from three or even four different angles, hence three or four different operators. He even had videos put together of innocent meetings at tech shows and weapons demos to demonstrate the power he possessed with his device. Even if they weren't guilty of deviant behavior, they sure in hell were scared of Trust's ability to watch every move they made without them being aware of it. I have seen a few of the DVDs, and let me tell you, it is some kind of impressive. Even the night videos are sharp and crisp. If there was any kind of light at all, his satellites picked it up."

"How did he get his satellites in space? I thought that they had to be approved by our government?" Briggs asked.

"We didn't put them up there. He used the Russians to put up his first ones. They were apparently cheaper. But he had a deal with them to share technology. All perfectly legal. Once the first satellite worked out, he put up another, but he needed more for the system to work perfectly. The system can also piggyback off drones for short, tight operations, but it's the satellites that really pull it together and work twenty-four seven. And satellites are a lot harder to detect than launching and recovering a drone that has to share airspace with other aircraft, not to mention the fact that drones can be easily tracked and shot down."

"So what's stopping him from launching these devices or selling them, or doing whatever he has planned?" Briggs asked.

"We are. We have the whole thing stalled right now." Check paused, looking down at a notebook in his lap.

"But you can't tell me anymore than that. Right?" Briggs replied sarcastically.

"Yeah, something like that. Sorry." Check looked away. Briggs thought he almost did look sorry. "Anyway, that's where Trust went off the deep end. When he couldn't get his device considered for the trial phase in order for it to be purchased by the military, he had the incriminating DVDs hand-delivered, along with a note which basically said, 'How could you not consider my device for trials? You just can't argue with results like this.' He had their faces blacked out and the audio altered, but they knew what they were seeing.

"The rest is an ongoing thing that we don't need to discuss. I have a hunch that maybe Trust is trying to make a deal with the Iraqis, and this might have something to do with it. The US government has stopped him cold, so he may be headed in another direction. Like I said, this is just part of the picture, not the whole story."

Check's man returned from the back of the plane with the phone Trust gave Briggs to keep and handed Check the other phone. He informed them that it contained a GPS tracking device that was locked in the on position that way Trust could follow his every move. They'd installed their own software so they could do the same. It did not have a listening device on it, however, so Briggs's conversations would not be monitored.

Check handed that phone to Briggs. "This one is for you. The other one," he pointed to the phone they had been examining, "can be given to Blake as his uncle requested." Check smirked.

Check spent the remainder of the long flight with Briggs, going over scenarios about Briggs's upcoming missions, along with his new duties for the Service. Check laid out a map of the Iraqi town Briggs would be working in and went over every safe area and street in detail.

CHAPTER EIGHTEEN

September 2006

Briggs jumped from the back seat of an up-armored Humvee onto the dusty ground that floated up around his ankles like talcum powder.

"Man, it's good to see you, Sarge!" Blake called out.

"Now there's a familiar sight," Briggs remarked as the dust settled back on his boots. Blake gave Briggs a friendly slap on the back as he assisted him with his gear.

"Everything been okay 'round here?" Briggs asked, looking around. His innate concern for the welfare of the men in his platoon overrode any other thought.

"All accounted for. Everyone has their fingers and toes. Man, it's good to see you. Welcome home to Iraq, where the action never stops, the food sucks, and everything blows up." Blake slapped him on the back again. Briggs grinned, nodding.

Over the next month, Briggs and Blake grew surprisingly close, considering their tenuous history. Their conversations always seemed to come back to Blake's Uncle Shelby, anticipating all the good times they would have when they returned home. Their combat rotation would screw them out of being home for Christmas, and they wouldn't return to the States until early next year, but they were okay with it. Other battalions would get to be home with their families, but at least Briggs's platoon would enjoy easier duties for a while, mostly training and base security.

There was the occasional combined operation out in the badlands, but mainly they stuck close to the operations base. They were able to Skype home every day to stay connected with loved ones. The atmosphere was extremely relaxed, and the Marines too, all except for Briggs. He couldn't let go of the inconsistencies in Check's description of Trust and his own and Blake's experiences with the man. What was the truth? What was he missing?

Since the day Briggs got back to Iraq, it seemed like Check was around him all the time, in one form or another. Even though they were discrete, Briggs was aware that Check's men were shadowing him, especially around Blake. After a while, he got used to it. What could he do about it? So he started to let up a little, relax just a smidgeon, and accept the reality of his new undercover life. The upside to this loss of privacy was a sense of security. There were lots of eyes on him, watching, waiting, and protecting. That meant all those around him were doubly protected too, and they didn't even know it. He even had a hunch that the light duty they were pulling was because Check had fixed it that way. Eventually, Briggs chose to look at the entire situation as a win-win, accepting that it was worth putting up with Check's constant surveillance if it kept his men at the lowest possible level of risk.

Late one night, Briggs was awakened by his cell phone buzzing. It was Check.

He told Briggs to get dressed and wait for one of his men to pick him up. Briggs was driven off the base in a small, white panel van with no windows and a sheet of plywood covering the back doors. He had seen it several times on the base. It was used to deliver local fruits and vegetables, along with the occasional freshly butchered goat or lamb. The only seats were for the driver and passenger in the front. The windshield was so horribly fractured, seeing through it seemed impossible. But the driver—a local—skillfully maneuvered through the dusty roads. The van stunk like a barnyard, and dried blood clung to the walls. Apparently, livestock was butchered right in the back. Or maybe something worse. Briggs didn't ask, but he did make a mental note to better scrutinize the food in the chow hall. The makeshift floorboard of plywood bounced up and down every time they hit a pothole.

Three of Check's goons were inside the back of the van, all armed to the teeth with serious non-government-issue hardware. Briggs noticed they all were carrying Glock .40 caliber pistols with extended magazines. It was the same type of pistol Check carried— apparently the chosen weapon of these high-end gunslingers who provided security for people at the upper levels of the food chain.

Check's men didn't say a word until the van came to a stop. One of them slid a section of plywood aside, exposing a rusted-out hole in the floor of the van just to the side of the drive shaft to the rear axle.

"Okay, jump down and watch your step," he said to Briggs.

Under the van was a steel door that opened downward into a passageway. Briggs started to swing his weapon over his shoulder to climb down the ladder when one of the men said, "Here, hand it to me, and I'll pass it down to you."

Briggs handed him the firearm, not giving it a second thought until he got to the bottom. A man pointed him down to the end of the shaft, where another was holding a blue-lens flashlight, showing the way. His heart picked up speed as he looked up, realizing that his weapon was not going to be handed down to him. The ladder was dragged upward and the door shut tight. Dust and small fragments of rock rained down on the floor of the passageway as Briggs heard the van rumble off, his weapon in it.

Damn it, should have seen that one coming.

He fumed for a few minutes, hands clenched tightly into fists, until his breathing slowed and he could reason out the situation. This must be their protocol. I'm not one of the boys . . . yet. You don't trust anyone outside of the club. Makes sense. Hell, I would have done the same thing.

He kept his mouth shut and followed the blue-lens flashlight along the passageway, all the while taking stock of his surroundings and everything he saw. He'd counted five of Check's men: three in the van and two in the tunnel. Their weapons were all short range, close-quarters type of firearms, which meant number six—their sniper—was somewhere on top with a long-range weapon. All the men he'd seen so far were wired with headsets, a radio antenna protruding out of the back shoulder pocket of their vests. They wore dark heavy pants, long-sleeved shirts, and baseball caps with small LED lights in the bill. The elbows and knees of their clothing had thick padding sewn in them, which helped them fall comfortably into a fighting position without needing pads strapped to their legs and arms. Their shirts, as well as their pants, were made of Kevlar—big-time expensive. They also wore black Danner combat boots with fighting knives tucked into them. Briggs could tell from their gear and their actions that these guys were high-speed professionals, picked for their exceptional talents. Briggs recognized these men. They had been on the same flight, but they hadn't spoken to him—not a word—during the entire eleven-hour journey to Iraq.

The men led him to a passageway with a tight spiral staircase at the end of it. His two escorts descended first, their boots making a metallic clicking sound on each metal step. Down, down, down. Briggs counted over twenty-five steps on his way to the bottom of the ladder well. His best estimate was that they were more than thirty-five or forty feet underground. When they reached the bottom, they entered another large passageway that had railcar tracks in the center of it, and Briggs had to be careful where he walked to keep from tripping.

One more right turn and they were out of the main passageway, and the tracks disappeared into the darkness behind him. He passed several small rooms along the corridor. Some had sturdy steel doors with large heavy hinges and locks. He could smell fresh paint. Reaching out, he lightly touched a door. The paint was still tacky. He counted six doors down the main hallway and six more as he and his escorts made a right turn down another passageway. Each door in this new passageway was bolted shut with two large padlocks, some type of double security requiring two people, or two keys. At the end of the second hallway, the men made another right turn to pass through back-to-back doors, both heavily guarded by more men in similar dress, carrying similar weapons.

Briggs didn't even bother to look at their faces at this point. He concentrated on his path. There was more light at the end of the second tunnel, but they were all red lights, like on a ship's overhead passageways.

"Okay, stop here," one of his escorts said. "Go through this door, wait until I close it, and the other door will open. Pass through it and the colonel will be waiting for you on the other side."

Briggs nodded and followed the instructions. The second door swung open, and he was hit by a bright light pouring in from a large, cavernous room with several large pillars supporting the ceiling above. Check sprung from a chair in front of a desk still wrapped in plastic.

"Sorry to yank you out of bed this late at night," he said. "Coffee?"

"No, but thanks," Briggs replied as he scanned the enormous room. It was full of boxes and crates, stacked to the ceiling in some spots. He estimated the room was as big as a football field with a ten-foot-high ceiling.

"Impressive, isn't it?" Check said as he leaned against the desk, the plastic crackling in protest. "This is just one of five such caverns we've discovered. Saddam Hussein and his henchmen squirreled away a lot of stuff. Everything in this place is brand new, from computers to tanks. The bigger items are in another location out in the desert. Some of these boxes are full of humanitarian aid sent during the embargo for the Iraqi people. If you notice the smell, that's fresh produce that was supposed to be delivered to schools and soup kitchens in the poorer neighborhoods. They just piled it up in here and let it spoil." Check looked out over the expansive hollow. "Fuckers."

Briggs noticed several flashes from a high-speed camera taking pictures on the other side of the wall of green plywood boxes. He nodded in that direction and lifted his eyebrows in question at Check.

"We're taking inventory of all of this to determine where it came from," Check explained. "It makes our job easier if the shipping crates aren't destroyed. Take a look at this picture."

On the desk was a photograph. Check slid it over for Briggs to take a look: a box with an odd icon on it.

"That little insignia is one of Trust Industry's marks. There are several of them in here."

This surprised Briggs, but he remained quiet, taking it all in. Check didn't mention what was in the boxes, and Briggs didn't bother asking. He knew that if he needed to know, they would tell him.

Check eyed Briggs for a reaction, and apparently seeing nothing, he continued the history of the stash. "I never did like working in supply, but that's where I was stuck for two years after getting wounded in Lebanon. It's paying off big time right now because I was able to find some similarities among all the chaos. The captain—let's call him Rex—who Hussein had assigned to hide all of this got the job because he had a photographic memory. He was instructed to never make a list of anything stored anywhere." Check pursed his lips, rocked back on his heels.

Briggs's eyes started to narrow.

"But he did make a list. Apparently he was going to sell the list to the US in exchange for his freedom and a nice home in the States. Saddam found out about it, of course."

Check pulled another chair up to the desk and indicated for Briggs to sit down. Check continued talking as he paced back and forth.

"So the deal was never closed. Our sources tell us that sometime in 2001, Hussein sent two of his most trusted men to pick up Rex." Check paused. "These two fine, upstanding gentlemen were Hussein's sons, Uday and Qusay. That set a lot of things in motion, especially when Daddy told his two most trusted psychopathic henchmen children to bring him the lowly bookkeeper with no books. They were told to take Rex to one of his little playhouses—not so fun for Rex though. Uday and Qusay knew well enough that no one came back from the playhouses.

"Now, being the greedy little sorts that they were, they knew Rex was worth big bucks to Daddy, so they decided to try to cash in for themselves. After all, if Daddy wanted this guy for some reason, then the sons knew they would want it as well." Check scoffed. "Distrust and dishonor: a family tradition."

Briggs nodded, trying to hide his impatience.

"When they arrived at Rex's house, they asked him a few questions while he was tied to a chair in the kitchen. They made themselves at home, drinking his hidden stash of wine and raping his wife and two daughters. Rex kept his mouth shut. Not a word. What the two of them were doing was nothing compared to what Saddam would do to him if he talked. Rex knew this. He held out for a long time, but eventually he broke. The bookkeeper of all the secrets not written down confessed that he had written them down and that he'd planned to sell the secrets to the United States."

"Is that what this is all about? Saddam's stash of ill-gotten goods?"

"You're getting there," Check replied, holding up a finger. "You see, Scott, we are looking for hidden weapons of mass destruction. Did you notice all the boxes with Chinese markings, and Russian ones too?"

Briggs had noticed, but a voice screamed inside his head, Bullshit. He was no dummy. If weapons of mass destruction were what Check and his men were really looking for, every one of them would be in hazmat suits, swabbing down boxes for trace elements. No, there was something else to this whole thing, something bigger. He was sure of it.

"The list. You're looking for Rex's list," he whispered.

"It would speed up the process."

"And Rex is dead?"

"Well, he's not around for us to ask him about the notebook. At one point in the friendly little conversation between Rex and the boys, Rex got a backbone. He decided to take them to 'the notebook' hidden in the walls of his office. Off they go to retrieve it, right? I mean, the sons figured Rex was surely telling the truth at this point, since they'd used the majority of his kitchen utensils to convince him to do so, if you know what I mean. But when they got to the office, the notebook was not to be found, and the sons had an epiphany that Rex had lied to them in order to get them away from his home, his family. That's when they tried to beat it out of him. He died in the process."

"So how did you find this place?" Briggs asked, figuring that he wouldn't get an answer.

"Rex's wife," Check blurted.

Startled by this new information, the wheels started spinning in Briggs's head. He was like a duck sitting on the water. His facial expression was sturdy and fixed, but he was paddling like hell beneath the surface.

"You're going to figure it out sooner or later." Check sat on the corner of the desk. "The deal Rex was making, to sell the list and come to the States with his family, was with me. I was put in charge of executing the deal. By the time Uday and Qusay figured out that Rex was lying, the wife had got on the satellite phone we'd given Rex. We got her out of there, along with the book. We were in the middle of putting the deal together when Saddam found out, and the whole thing blew up in our faces. Are you following this?"

"I think so," Briggs said. "You thought Saddam's WMDs would be revealed in the notebook."

"More importantly, we hoped to find them before the war started, to add to our justification for invading. WMDs make a certain group of people shut up very quickly and a president and his war machine look justified."

"So have you found the WMDs yet?"

"Not so fast. I haven't finished my story."

Briggs exhaled a frustrated breath and ran his fingers through his hair.

"Ah come on, it's a good story." Check started to pace back and forth once again. "Now the wife wants to play the game. She tells my guys who got her and her daughters out of the apartment that she knows where the other notebooks are hidden. But first she wants to go to America. And she wants to drag along her entire family, right down to her damn grandfather—all before she will tell us. Of course we tell her 'hell no' and lean on her, saying we already knew where most of the notebooks were, just not all of them. We tell her if she will give us the books, we will put her and her daughters on a flight out that night. She agrees and pulls a notebook from underneath her burqa." Check slapped the desk. "Ha! How about that? She had it on her the entire time." He walked to the far end of the desk and placed his hands on the corner of it to stretch out his back.

Briggs could hear voices at the far end of the storage room and could still see the occasional camera flash. "So did you get all the books?"

"No. We just got the one she had on her, and we know she didn't have any others. My guys moved her and her daughters to a safe house and started to gather up the rest of her family to get them out of Iraq. She was told to stay put while we verified the location of one of the caches on the other side of town—just like this one, only a little smaller. There are a total of twelve of these caches, and we've only found five so far. Using the book that came from the wife, I found some clues that gave away the other locations. My guys were all Iraqi nationals serving as double agents, so gathering intel was fairly easy. They were extremely patriotic and wanted to build a better Iraq after the war they knew was coming."

Check paused for a long period before he began again. "When my guys returned to the safe house after verifying the first stash, something happened. I think they were followed, or an informant ratted them out. I'm not sure. A firefight broke out and someone tossed a grenade in the room with Rex's wife. So now she's gone, and all we have is the one notebook."

He pointed at Briggs. "Hence the reason we recruited you." Check looked at Briggs narrowly. "Trust knows the location of the other stash houses."

"What? How do you know that?"

"Take a look at this." Check handed Briggs a small device. It was cylindrical, like a cigar holder, only thinner. "So far, we have found twenty-four of these hidden in various places among the boxes here. Some are marked Russian, some are marked Chinese, and some from Trust Industries, but all with the same type of device putting out the same encrypted location signal."

Briggs tried to control the explosion in his head as the evidence being presented to him revealed the bad side of Trust that Check had been warning him about. A side Briggs hadn't seen and had begun to believe wasn't there.

"If he knows where all the stash houses are, then why don't you just ask him?"

"We can't trace a single thing back to him. All the devices are encrypted with a cancellation code."

"What does that mean?"

"It means these devices only put out a signal for a very short distance, say a maximum of a hundred and fifty feet. If we use any type of interrogation device to pick up the signals, they shut down. All you get is one little ping, faint enough to sound like all the other little pings you get from a multitude of false signals."

Briggs was trying to make sense of everything he was hearing. How could he have been so fooled by Trust? Then his thoughts shifted to Trust's nephew. "So how does Jeff Blake tie into all of this?"

"He has had a passive tracking device on him ever since he's been in country. It gathers location data everywhere he goes, and he has been damn near everywhere, walking, riding, and flying."

"Maybe he doesn't know he has it," Briggs said hopefully.

"Oh, he knows he has it, all right. It looks just like a cell phone. Just like the new one you gave him as a gift from his uncle. Every couple of weeks, Blake hands it off to one of his uncle's guys, and they download the data from it. But we discovered that Blake stopped handing off the phone a few weeks back. We think they found it. That is why they stopped the handoffs."

"Well, he must be pretty slick with the handoffs because I've never seen him do it."

"Neither have we, and we have tried to catch him at it, believe me. There is a good chance that he has been sending them wirelessly, but we're not sure."

Check's eyes were wide with excitement as he picked up the tracking device from the desk and handed it to Briggs, who rolled it around in his hands thoughtfully. He wished the old guy would get to the point of exactly what he was doing there and what it was they wanted him to do, but he also knew there was an art to delivery and Check thought himself a master narrator. Check was on a roll and had started to drop little hints of information, clues that Briggs filed away in his brain.

Information is power.

Such as the power in the one little word that Check had let slip out during his storytelling. The word "it." He'd said, "We think they found it."

The burning question now was: what was it?

Check's song and dance about finding the WMDs in order to justify the war and vindicate the president was a beautifully orchestrated expression of patriotism. But something was going on just under Check's words.

It. What could "it" be?

Whatever it was, Briggs was getting the sense that it had turned into a personal obsession for Check.

Briggs pointed toward a pile of boxes. "How did Trust get his shipments in here in the first place?" he asked, a frown deepening the lines on his forehead.

"He knows how Hussein operated. A lot of the boxes are old, from more than ten years ago when trade was a wide-open market. Most of the large crates are spare parts that support oil drilling and other oil-processing operations. You see, Trust's people who worked here long before the war started knew Hussein was skimming off the top and blatantly stealing. I told you—Trust is smart."

Briggs nodded his head, chewing on his lip.

"And here is a testimony to how smart Trust is." Check spread out his arms and motioned to all the items in the room. "He knew Hussein was hiding away everything he could steal, and he also knew he was amassing enormous amounts. Now you can never get a squirrel to tell you where he hides his nuts, and if that squirrel sees you watching him bury the nut, he'll just dig it up and hide it somewhere else. So, Trust started bugging the nut."

Check rubbed his eyes and spoke in a slower, more controlled fashion. "I need you to confront Blake and ask for his help. He is the connection to Trust, and if Blake will help us, we will wash the whole thing."

"Wash?"

"We won't put Blake in Leavenworth for spying."

Briggs head spun.

Spying? That's what Check is asking me to do, Briggs thought. Good God! Is this what I have to look forward to? Would prison time be my thanks for working for the Service? Living in a dark rat hole, questioning everything to the point of total paranoia? Briggs didn't want to be like Check, like this.

Out of all the spy novels and action thrillers he'd ever read, not one of them had gotten even close to the real truth behind the business of the military. Briggs was beginning to feel that a steady flow of lies—constant lies about everything—was the norm. "Need to know" was a mantra, a sign of superiority over those who did not "need to know." The phrase made Briggs sick—with anxiety, with disgust, with frustration—every time he heard it.

But he had gleaned one thing finally: he was quite certain that this mission was for Check's benefit. Somehow, "it" was all about him.

Briggs took a deep breath and tried to put on his best poker face. "Okay, so how do you suggest I approach Blake?"

Over the next thirty minutes, Check ran through the particulars of what Briggs could say to Blake. Briggs was then taken back to the base in a different vehicle. His weapon was lying on the seat.

On the ride back, his mind swirled with the information he had been given about Trust and his growing suspicions of Check. What exactly was he in the middle of? Whom could he believe? At this point, he wasn't sure.

CHAPTER NINETEEN

October 2006

Briggs arrived at the base just before what would have normally been reveille, but it was the weekend, so all those off duty were sleeping in. The chow hall was open, so Briggs made his way over to it, following the smell of freshly made coffee and bacon. After last night's ride in what he now called the "gut wagon," he had his doubts about the bacon, but he was hungry so he filled his plate and walked across the open dining area. There was only a handful of Marines scattered about. Jeff Blake was eating alone at the end of a sea of empty tables.

Briggs's steps slowed as he walked toward Blake. How deeply was he embedded in his uncle's business? How much did he know?

"You're up early," Briggs said as he placed his tray across from Blake.

Blake glanced up at Briggs and smiled. The table was next to one of the industrial-sized ice machines in the far back corner. The noise from it was deafening at times, as the compressor constantly hummed and the cubes of ice clattered in the collection bin every few minutes.

"Couldn't you have found a better place to sit?" Briggs asked, raising his voice slightly to be heard.

"I could have, but this is the best place for us to talk right now. No one will sit with us here."

"What the hell are you talking about?" Briggs asked. *Does he know?*

Blake pulled his phone from his pocket and tapped it with his fingers, indicating that the noise of the ice machine would make it difficult for them to be heard. As he slid it back into his pocket, Briggs drew in a short, choppy breath. The ice was broken for their unavoidable conversation, in an appropriate place, and Briggs hadn't even had to start it.

"Are you sure?" Briggs asked, tapping his finger on his pocket that held his own cell phone.

Over the last several weeks Briggs had been feeling that the phone had become a tether to his master, and when the leash was jerked, Briggs obeyed. Now he was ready to exercise more control, his "need to know" space having been significantly increased by Check's recent revelations, both intentional and unintentional.

"Yes, I have tried it from my end. He hates it when I sit here."

He. Briggs assumed it was Trust, and in a flash of realization, he knew that Blake was getting tired of his master as well.

"So, we can speak freely?"

"Pretty much. Just don't get too loud, and when the icemaker cycle ends, start eating. It will start up again in about forty-five seconds. Whatever you do, don't take the battery out of your phone. They will know what we're up to. I've already tried that too."

"What *are* we up to, Blake?" Briggs asked.

"We are saving the world from the axis of evil. Don't you know that? You and I are pawns in a game that is so big, it is mind-blowing. After we kill all the people here, we are going to go somewhere else and do the same thing. You get that, right?"

The ice machine finished its cycle, and the ice fell like thunder. Then the noise dwindled to a soft, low hum. Blake picked up his fork and began to eat his scrambled eggs without breaking his gaze from Briggs. Briggs returned the stare for a brief moment and then stood. He walked over to a large, glass-front refrigerator and removed two small containers of milk. He returned to the table and passed one to Blake.

"Thanks, man." Blake took a long drink, until a loud thump announced the beginning of the next cycle of ice-making.

"What are you doing for Trust, Blake?"

"The same thing you're doing for your people—helping to end the war, of course."

"That's the standard answer, Blake. I need something more specific."

"You need? You don't need anything! It's whoever is pulling your strings that needs. Let me put a little question in your head that you need to answer for yourself. What are you getting out of this roller-coaster ride? You see, I know it has been harder on you than it has been on me. That is one of the reasons I never wanted any authority to deal with. I'm just along for the ride. The only person I worry about is me. It's less complicated that way."

"I thought all you cared about was getting your ass stuffed into a body bag?"

"I've had a change of heart. I guess you could say I've set a new goal—one I'm looking forward to attaining." Blake drank the rest of his milk. "Your food is getting cold. What's wrong, not hungry anymore?" he said sarcastically.

Briggs glared at him.

"You see, this doesn't bother me at all. I have a healthy appetite, and Trust doesn't give me a hard time. I shoot bad guys during the day and sleep well at night, unlike you. I don't have to sneak off the base at night to attend clandestine meetings and get orders from *my* master."

The fact that Blake knew he was working for someone and he'd spent the night off base talking to Check could only mean one thing: someone in Check's confidence had informed Trust, who let Blake know. It was obvious that Blake's network of information was larger than Check's; however, Briggs did not let it faze him. At this level in the game, certain things were not important. But some things were. And Briggs had had enough.

"Bullshit! Blake, you're a fool. In my pocket, I have a picture of my girlfriend, her daughter, and my entire family, along with the first letters she ever sent me. All neatly tucked away in a Ziploc bag behind the hard plate on my body armor, so if it has to be returned to my family, it won't be soaked in blood. I have one of my dad's dog tags on my keychain that I am never without." Briggs stopped abruptly as the ice machine ended its cycle again. This time, he ate his eggs and what he hoped was bacon.

Blake twisted uncomfortably in his seat and adjusted the sling on the weapon on his back. The noise started again and so did Briggs.

"All you have is an enormous amount of guilt for a heinous sin you committed and that damn journal with a bullet hole in it. Your life is all about death, man. Hell, you're not even brave enough to seek forgiveness for your sin. You're just going to die with it and let your soul drag it around for eternity. Here is something you need to think about, Jeff Blake." Briggs stabbed at his eggs and held the forkful in the air. "I care enough to make sure those who love me don't have to suffer any more than they have to— particularly if it comes to my death—by the simple act of placing these items I know will be returned to them in this fucking Ziploc bag. That little act goes a long way in the form of compassion for those who will mourn my loss. That's my moral compass. I look out for the people around me. Blake, are you trading your moral compass for a promise of part of your uncle's dynasty?"

Briggs's words seemed to strike a nerve in Blake, who slowly pushed himself away from the table and stood.

"I can see this conversation is going nowhere," Blake said, then turned and headed toward the barracks.

Briggs followed, a short five strides behind him. The conversation was not over. Blake's next move, however, was somewhat drastic. Briggs watched as Blake pressed the reset button on his phone several times. If Trust's people were anything like Check's, this probably meant that he was activating some kind of emergency signal or that Trust's team of men was now tracking Blake's location via the cell phone.

Briggs caught up with Blake in the rec room of the barracks.

"Tell me, what's going on?"

"Why should I tell you anything?" Blake asked.

"Because I am your friend and this has gotten out of hand. If you don't tell me what's going on, I can't help you."

Blake sat down and fidgeted nervously in his chair. Briggs guessed that he might really want to talk, but he was fighting it. He wanted to give Blake a little more time to come clean, but Check had pushed him hard to gather information.

"I know that Shelby wants you to do something for him, and knowing him and how he is, it has got to be something big. So, tell me what it is." Briggs's voice was stronger and more demanding now.

"What? You don't know my uncle. Just because you went fishing with him a few times doesn't make you an authority on Shelby Trust, so don't come off like I owe you. I don't." Blake stood up again to leave the room.

"Sit your ass down!" Briggs ordered. "This conversation is not over."

"Oh, what, you're pulling rank on me now, Sergeant?"

"Yeah, if that's what it takes."

"It's not that easy," Blake replied as he began to pace back and forth.

Now that the two of them were away from the cover of the noisy ice machine in the chow hall, Briggs knew Check had heard every word through the cell phone in his pocket. He knew his options were gone, and now he would have to pull Blake out of play. Hoping he would give up Trust was all they had left.

Briggs's phone vibrated in his pocket. He quickly reached in and silenced the rattling. He knew it was Check calling him with orders on what to do with Blake, but Briggs's blood was boiling and the pressure from Check set him off even more. He was on the verge of losing his temper. The thought of throwing the phone on the floor and stomping it into silence crossed his mind. He turned to focus his anger back on Blake, but he had walked out of the room. He screamed for Check's benefit, "Give me a damn minute, will you?"

Blake had returned to his room in the barracks and closed the door behind him. Briggs needed time to think, so he did the same just a few doors down, but not so far away that he couldn't hear if Blake's door opened. He knew Blake could not use his phone because Check's satellite block was still in place, so he would not be able to get word to Trust that they were on to him.

Again, his phone vibrated. "Damn it, get off me, Colonel. I need time to think, and I swear if you don't back off, I will take the butt of my rifle to this phone." The phone stopped vibrating immediately and Briggs responded, "Thank you," into the dead air. The answers that Check wanted were all locked up in Blake's head, and Briggs had just shown his hand. There wasn't much more he could do if Blake wasn't going to come clean. He reached into his pocket and dialed Check.

"It's time to bring him in, Scott," Check said quickly. "He's not going to tell you anything, so we'll have to do this my way now."

"What do you mean *your way*?" The question was rhetorical of course. Briggs knew Blake would undergo interrogation and possibly worse. Because they were in Iraq, Check would turn Blake over to the Iraqi intelligence division, and they would perform the task of interrogation. If they got the information they wanted, all the better. But either way, it was a sure bet that Blake would wind up dead. He would be just another Marine captured in a firefight, killed in battle. It could all be arranged so quickly and easily, and no one would be the wiser. Check also had all the proof he needed to label Blake a spy, which meant that if he did survive, he'd have a one-way ticket to Fort Leavenworth, or worse, Guantanamo Bay. No matter how it went, it was obvious to Briggs that Blake would never see the light of day again unless he helped Check right now.

With those thoughts in mind, Briggs asked for one more try at Blake. But the wheels were already in motion.

"It's too late," Check said firmly. "I have three men on their way."

Briggs flung open his door just in time to see three men, each over six feet tall and dressed in light-brown cargo pants with matching shirts and ball caps, armed with short M4 automatic weapons, Glock side arms, and sling-style cartridge belts, force their way into Blake's room.

"No! Hey!" Briggs shouted down the long hall of the building, void of people except for Check's three goons. It was too late. Check's men disarmed Blake and forced him down on to his rack to place zip tie cuffs on him.

"Get your damn hands off him! You can't walk him out of this compound in cuffs like a damn criminal." Briggs shook with anger.

Blake was totally motionless with his hands hanging down by his side.

"Just give me a damn minute with the Marine," Briggs said, almost pleading, as he pulled Blake from the rack and to the other side of the room. Check's men stood with their weapons trained on the two of them. He noticed that they were wearing earpieces with radios strapped to their backs. "Tell him to give me a few minutes, okay? Just tell him." When no one moved, he yelled, "Tell him!"

One of the men nodded at Briggs and acknowledged the radio call from Check. "He said you have two minutes."

"Fine, go down to my room and close the door. I don't want anyone to see you hanging out in the hall. You obviously don't fit in." Even though all three appeared to be Marines, their gear and weapons were not standard issue. They would raise suspicions if they were seen in the hallway. Check apparently told his men to cooperate because they exited the room after some long glares.

Briggs looked at Blake. His eyes were wide and bright; his expression had changed. Blake lifted his index finger to his lips, pulled a pen from his pocket, and wrote something on the palm of his hand. He held it up for Briggs to read, then just as quickly, he wiped it off by rubbing his palm vigorously on his pants leg.

He'd written: "Check?"

Briggs felt faint, the color rushing from his face, barely able to keep his knees from buckling beneath him. It was the same feeling he'd had when he was buried in the dark basement of the building, clutching the Jordanian who had spoken in perfect English: "Please don't kill me."

The confusion of that moment in the basement during battle came rushing back to Briggs as did all the questions.

What have I done?

Who is the bad guy?

Why was Blake asking about Check now?

"What the—?" was all he could think to say aloud, taking a step back as if Blake were ablaze.

What parts are we all playing in this game?

How many games are we playing?

The questions kept rolling in his head.

Blake motioned to Briggs; he wanted the cell phone in Briggs's pocket. Briggs froze in confusion as Blake took it, returned to the rack, and removed his own cell phone from his pocket, placing them under the pillow on his bed. He motioned to Briggs to move to the other side of the small room, sat down very close to him, and spoke in a low voice.

"I am working for Shelby, but not in the way you seem to think I am. You have to let me get out of here. Shelby is working for the government just like Check is, and if those three dudes take me out of here, they will all wind up missing, along with me. My uncle will see to that."

"What the hell is going on Blake? Is it the WMDs? Have you found them?" Briggs whispered.

"WMDs? You have got to be kidding me. Is that what Check told you?"

Briggs nodded. "I've seen one of the underground stashes of goods that Saddam Hussein has hidden away. Is that what this is all about?"

"Check is playing you for a fool, Scott. Shelby doesn't give a shit about all that stuff or WMDs. He is looking for something far more important and valuable than a bunch of junk in an Iraqi shithole. And I've got a hunch that Check is looking for it as well."

It.

"You have to tell me what *it* is," Briggs said, grabbing Blake's arm tightly and shaking him.

Blake seemed to be weighing his options. Briggs warned, "Don't fuck with me now, man. It is *not* the time."

Blake nodded. "Okay, but I just don't want you dead, okay? If you tell Check what I'm about to tell you, and I'm right about Check like I think I am, you will wind up dead. Because I'm sure Check is after what my uncle is after, and Check will stop at nothing to get it."

"What about your uncle?"

Blake did not answer. An uneasy silence followed.

Briggs gritted his teeth and shook Blake again. "Tell me. What is it they are looking for? Just tell me. I'll make my own decisions from there."

Blake blurted, "Gold! Not just a little gold, but thousands of pounds of gold. All that crap hidden away and all the oil that was sold before the embargo and even after the embargo, Hussein turned into gold. Any cash he received, he had converted to gold on foreign trading markets. He wasn't paid in cash. He was paid in gold. More gold than you could move with a bulldozer. And I'm telling you, Check wants it for himself. If you let the cat out of the bag, you will find out exactly where Check's loyalties lie. Think about it, Scott, if you tell Check about this conversation and you're wrong about him, you're dead. If you keep your mouth closed, you live, and you can help us—me and my uncle, the good guys— recover the gold. Check thinks you're some type of uneducated backwater hick and you won't question too much what goes on. That way he can use you to get what he wants. And it's working so far."

Briggs's mind reeled. If everything Blake said was true, his family was at risk now for sure. His home was still being monitored by Check; his life was being controlled by Check. He had no idea what to do. What was he? A Marine? Or a secret operative? Whom did he work for? How would he ever know for sure . . . until it was too late?

"What the hell am I going to do?"

"You've got to let me go, Scott, and you've got to keep your mouth shut. You can help us if you like, or just stay out of it. That's up to you. But if you talk to Check, you're as good as dead. Do you understand?"

"How . . . ?" Briggs couldn't even get a question out. He gripped his head in his hands, trying to contain all the information and formulate a plan.

Blake said, "I can't tell you any more, okay, except that the signals you and Check thought you were blocking were *not* blocked. And without a doubt whatsoever, Shelby has activated an extraction for me. He has a lot more power and pull than you can imagine, and I don't mean just with the American government."

For the first time in his life, Scott Briggs was lost. No strategies or game plans popped into his head, and all his thoughts were blank. He just stood there motionless, waiting to see what would happen next. In just about thirty seconds, Check's men would return and there would be no stopping them this time. They would take Blake away, probably him as well, and an entirely new game would start with no leeway or tolerance for unanswered questions.

"All I am asking is for you to let me go before Check's men come back. I will be out that window and out of here in three seconds." Blake pointed to six Iraqi soldiers who were standing by a panel truck forty feet away. "Look. There is my ride. No one will get hurt. Just let me go." The extraction team was made up of Iraqi soldiers loyal to Trust, and it would not take them long to get him off the base. Blake walked over to the rack and reached under the pillow.

"Don't move, or I'll drop you Blake!" Briggs said in a low, commanding voice. Briggs had swung his rifle from around his back and sights were leveled on Blake.

"Be cool. I just need my phone." Blake slid his hand from under the pillow with just his cell phone. "Relax. I'm going now." He slowly walked over to the open window that had a thin eight-inch ledge with a twelve-foot drop to the ground. "I'm going now, so don't shoot me. I swear to you, I'm not a bad guy."

"No!" Briggs yelled. Blake had swung his legs out of the

window and was standing with his toes on the ledge beneath the window, his chest against the barrel of Briggs's weapon. Briggs stood rigid, rifle firmly pointed at Blake.

Blake's voice was calm. "We still have a lot to talk about, man, but right now I have to go. This will all work itself out, if you let me go. Just be cool." He then turned to look at the ground so he could see his landing spot, and glanced once more at Briggs.

Briggs could hear Check's men running down the hall, their boots stomping on the floor like a staggered drumbeat as they approached. He was frozen in his thoughts, but his finger had cleared the trigger guard and was poised in position. One quick pull and Blake would be dead before he completed his drop to the dirt below.

"Damn you, Blake! Get your ass back in the room, or I swear I will drop you!"

Briggs was angrier than he had ever been in his life because he was in the precarious position of threatening to kill a friend. But his voice was controlled and direct. He was capable of pulling the trigger if he had to.

"I gotta go now," Blake said and wiggled his fingers in farewell. "Oh, and the next time you see Check, ask him how your old man died. The answer will change your perspective."

Blake's last statement caused Briggs to jerk in confusion, lifting his head from the sights.

"Cancer! He died of cancer!" Briggs yelled as Blake jumped from the ledge.

Just then, the door was forcibly flung open, striking him in the shoulder, and causing him to discharge his weapon. The round bounced off the side of the window, sending brick and splinters of wood flying into the street. Briggs lost his balance and fell to the floor where the first of Check's men dove on him and removed his weapon. The second man covered both Briggs and the man who was holding him down. The third man ran to the window and turned back to Briggs. "Where the hell is he?"

Check's men quickly looked around the room and in the closet before they turned their attention to the street. There was no one there. Blake had disappeared along with the truck and armed Iraqis.

"Sir, our man has gone out the window and disappeared."

A truck, with Blake tucked safely inside, made its way off the compound unimpeded, fading into the early-morning traffic of automobiles and people.

CHAPTER TWENTY

October 2006

Briggs had been disarmed and was zip tie cuffed to a chair that had been slid into a corner. The chair legs were lashed to a pole so it could not be flipped over or moved. His legs had also been lashed to the legs of the chair. There was a cut below his left eye on his cheekbone, still oozing blood onto his collar. Check's men stood back from Briggs with their weapons trained on him, and no one spoke a word when Check entered the barracks.

Briggs watched Check survey the situation: two of the three men had bloody faces, and the third had his arm pushed into his half-zipped jacket up to his elbow. Without a word to them, Check picked up a handheld radio and called in to base ops.

"Base, this is Victor 3. I'm calling in a Full Court Press, over."

Full Court Press was the code name to lock down the entire base and muster all personnel that were in the perimeter, as well as to secure all VIP and visitors in the command bunker.

The call came back to Check. "Victor 3. Verify Full Court Press, over."

This was simply a formality; the lockdown had started.

"Roger, base, this is Victor 3. Full Court Press verify, over."

The call came back quickly, and Check informed them that they were looking for Jeff Blake who was AWOL, armed, and dangerous.

In his gut, Briggs knew Blake was long gone.

Briggs could hear people scrambling all over the base. He knew every door and every window was manned after the troop musters. All secure buildings were locked and tagged with a double guard standing at each and every post.

"What the hell happened to you?" Check turned to the man with his arm in a makeshift sling.

"Broken rib or two, thanks to him," he replied, pointing the M-4 he was holding toward Briggs, who was taking deep breaths and trying unsuccessfully to hold in his anger.

"And when I get out of this chair, I'm going to go to work on the other side!" Briggs spat.

Check's radio sounded off just then. "Victor 3, Victor 3, Charlie Oscar needs you at command center, over."

"Roger, I am on my way," Check said into the radio. He turned to his bloodied men and told them to report to their mustering point as he retrieved Briggs's weapons from one of them. "You're lucky he didn't get his hands on this," he said as he held up Briggs's twelve-inch K-bar.

After they left the room, he turned to Briggs and used the knife to cut his hands loose from the chair.

"Are you all calmed down now?"

"Yes, sir," Briggs replied as he took the knife Check held out to him and leaned over to cut away the lashings at his feet. Check grabbed a green towel from the end of the rack and offered it to Briggs. It was the only object in the room that had not been scattered on the floor during what had been one hell of a fight. Briggs took it and pressed down hard on his cheek to stop the bleeding.

"Thank you, sir." Briggs concealed his confusion with military protocol. After his conversation with Blake, Briggs's senses were on high alert. More than ever, he was unsure of who could be trusted.

"Damn, Scott, you just beat the shit out of three of my biggest badasses. Two of those guys are former SEALS. You probably hurt their pride more than their bodies." Check let out a chuckle as he pulled Briggs's hand away in order to inspect his cut.

"Well, their egos can't be bruised that much. I still wound up tied to this chair." He turned his face toward the ceiling in order for Check to get a better look at the cut.

"Yep, that's going to need stitches, my friend. Tell me what happened with Blake." Check's demeanor was calm as he sat on the edge of the rack.

"I'm sorry, Colonel. I just couldn't shoot him," Briggs explained matter-of-factly as he searched the bed for his phone. "He made it sound as if he were on some kind of parallel mission to mine and distracted me by saying something about my father's death. He told me to ask you about it, said it would change my perspective, whatever the hell that means." He realized his phone had fallen to the ground and snatched it from the floor. "What did he mean, sir?"

Before Check could respond, the radio sounded off, requesting Check's presence at the command center again. He ignored it.

"Yes, Scott, there is more to your father's death, and I will tell you all I know later. Right now, you have to give me all you can about Blake. I know it will be hard to do, but please concentrate on your last conversation with him. We will have all the time in the world to talk about your father when this is over."

Briggs frowned, his eyes narrowing as anger surged through his body. Damn it! It was his father they were talking about. He was sick of waiting for answers. He wanted to know now. But his military training kept him silent. He nodded his head and did his best to relay everything about Shelby Trust and the operation that Blake had told him. However, he left out the conversation about the gold. He would have to figure out what to do with that tidbit later.

"Are you pissed at me for letting him go?" Briggs asked with sincerity.

"No, don't be ridiculous. I didn't want you to kill him. Besides, he can't go far. We'll pick him up. Right now, you need to come with me to the command post so we can tie this all together. Now you know this changes things, right?"

"How's that, sir?"

"This operation, as far as you're concerned, is over. We have to get you out of the country and back home so you can start your training at Quantico."

"So I screwed it up."

"Not at all. You performed exceptionally, and the information you've gathered is going to help us immensely. I'll be talking to you later. The only thing that's over is this part of the operation."

A few days later, Check had Briggs removed from the base and flown to Camp Geiger, North Carolina. Check told him that he would be sent to Quantico in a month or so to start his training in the finer arts of surveillance and espionage in order to fulfill other missions with the Service. His first training session would take a little longer than eight months, and from there he would spend another three months training in Florida. How Briggs would explain his drastic change of plans to Anita swirled around in his head like a slowly approaching hurricane.

CHAPTER TWENTY-ONE

November 2006

When Briggs arrived at Camp Geiger, North Carolina, he spent a week being secretly processed out of the Marine Corps. His biggest secret was that he had a friend of his take his car out of storage and get it ready for him so he could drive home and surprise everyone. He didn't want to give his mother the opportunity to plan a big welcome home reception. He would simply slide in under the radar and meet his friends and family one at a time. Secrecy was part of his life now, and he didn't know if he would ever get used to it, because secrecy meant lies.

It was an extremely underwhelming and sterile operation. There would be no band, no retirement ceremony, no grand parade, no speech made in his honor. He was simply handed a stack of papers, an envelope with his new orders, and a note requesting his presence in the sergeant major's office.

On the designated day at 1200 sharp, he arrived at the battalion office dressed in his short sleeve Charlie uniform. He entered the foyer at the base headquarters and announced himself to the duty sergeant. The duty sergeant then invited him to have a seat. He had his pick of several chairs and ornate sofas that surrounded the entranceway to the base commander's office. They were all lush and looked very comfortable.

No way, Briggs thought to himself. *I am going to stay on my feet in case I have to make a break for it.* It was a little personal joke that helped him relax.

As soon as the thought flashed in his mind the base sergeant major Bradley Prafke appeared with his hand extended and a huge grin painted across his face. *Shit, this guy is tall,* Briggs thought.

"Good afternoon!" He said as he quickly closed the distance between the two of them and extended his hand to Briggs. "It is the afternoon, isn't it?" He lifted his left wrist and checked his watch. "Yep it is."

"Good afternoon, Sgt. Major." Briggs replied as he reached out and clasped the sergeant major's hand in his.

Prafke towered over Briggs at better than six foot two. His legs were so long it had only taken him three or four strides to close the distance between the two of them from his office to where Briggs was standing. Briggs noticed that part of his right ear was missing. He had several jagged scars on his shaven head that reflected so much ambient light it was almost blinding. He was in such awe of him that he forgot to let go of the sergeant major's hand until he focused on the enormous stack of ribbons above his left breast pocket. Prafke sensed he was uneasy.

"Nervous?"

"Yes, sir, I am."

"Why are you so nervous?" he questioned.

"I'm nervous because I don't know what to be nervous about."

Prafke cocked his head to one side and flashed a mischievous grin, this time with his eyes squinted. "That's good. You will do just fine."

What is he talking about? Briggs head was spinning with confusion and apprehension at the same time.

"Everything will make sense in a few minutes. I don't want to steal anyone's thunder here, so come on and find out." He motioned for Briggs to follow him down the corridor that led to the base commanding general's office.

Briggs felt as if the walls were closing in on him as he followed the sergeant major and tried to keep up with his massive strides. His mind was in full spin as he kept his eyes focused on the shoulders of the sergeant major.

A short distance down the long hallway, the sergeant major turned back to Briggs and said. "By the way I served with your father. He and I worked together."

Damn, I can't keep up with all of this. Served with my dad? In the Marine Corps or the service? Better not ask, he thought to himself. *Too much to process right now.*

When the two of them entered the commanding general's office, Briggs was surprised to see Master Gunnery Sergeant Hager waiting for him, as was Check. Check was dressed in Charlies as well. The sergeant major closed the door behind them. The staff had been dismissed for lunch, and the entire building was quiet. It was just the four of them now.

Check's presence, along with the sergeant major and Top Hager, made Briggs feel less tense. He sensed this would be the validation he had been seeking. No longer would he be unsure of his new role with the Service. Each of the three high-ranking Marines took turns shaking Briggs's hand and telling them how proud they were of him, but not one of them told him why he was there. That was the burning question in his mind, and he was about to explode when the door behind him opened, and a two-star general he had never seen before walked in the door.

"Attention on deck," said the sergeant major.

"At ease, gentlemen," the general said in a calm, pleasant voice.

He approached Briggs directly. "Major General Mitchell Bell. It is a pleasure to finally meet you, young man," he said as he extended his hand to Briggs. "I am sorry for all the cloak-and-dagger secrecy, but you are now a member of a very silent service, and when I say silent, I mean extremely secretive. We are all," he swept his arm around the room, "members of the service that you have been so diligently working for—rather blindly, as I understand. I am impressed with your abilities and your confidence. Unfortunately, for those of us who are members of this esteemed service, there are no parades blowing in the rafters and no notifications in the papers trumpeting our accolades—or in this case, yours." He paused, then bellowed, "Call to orders!"

The men came to attention, and the sergeant major stepped from behind his desk holding a red binder with the Marine Corps emblem embossed in gold in the center of it. Lying on top of the folder was a light blue jewelry case, and in it, the Silver Star. The sergeant major read the citation aloud. It was from the commandant of the Marine Corps and signed by the president of the United States, awarding Sergeant Scott Briggs the Silver Star with combat V for his actions in Iraq during the rescue of Lieutenant Adams.

Briggs struggled to keep his composure. Receiving a Silver Star was an important moment for him, and he wished his father were there to see it.

The conversation afterward was brief. The room was called to attention and General Bell exited as ceremoniously as he'd entered, but first leaned over to Check and said, "I'll see you after graduation."

Check exited the office next. Briggs laughed to himself. It was as if they had all been caught in a bank robbery and now were in a hurry to get into the wind.

He looked at the Silver Star and let loose a loud sigh.

Finally, he thought to himself, *there are faces in this crazy nightmare. I have something tangible, not just the word of one man.*

Top Hager placed his hand on Briggs's shoulder and led him out of the sergeant major's office.

"Colonel Check wanted me to sit down with you and tell you about your father. I should be the one to tell you because I was with him when it happened."

Briggs was incredibly confused, because he had watched his father fade away as cancer invaded his body, slowly robbing him of his life. How could the truth be any different from what he knew?

"I don't understand," Briggs said quietly.

"I know, but right now it's not the time to go into the details. I will come to your house where you and I and your mother can talk about it together. Trust me, it will be better that way."

With that, he shook Briggs's hand one more time and wished him well, promising to see him soon and answer all his questions.

Briggs stood quietly for several minutes wondering if his mother knew that there was more to his father's death than cancer. Questions loomed large in his thoughts and emotions. It seemed as though the more he wanted answers, the more he was deluged with questions.

CHAPTER TWENTY-TWO

November 2006

"Time for some entertainment in a can, boys."

The beer did its work and numbed the pain of a long day of training at Camp Geiger, igniting countless conversations, meaningful and meaningless, that flowed into the night. Briggs entered the room after several cans of entertainment had been consumed by the half dozen Marines gathered in one of the two-bunk rooms in the barracks.

"Sergeant Briggs, sir. Where you comin' from?" Matt Williams asked.

"Stop calling me sir, Williams. I work for a living just like you," Briggs replied, even though he knew Williams used the term out of respect.

"Have a beer?" Williams offered good-naturedly, his white-toothed grin lighting up the room, his voice tender compared to his massive bulk. He extended a cool can toward Briggs, and another Marine moved to offer his seat to the sergeant.

Briggs plucked the beer from Williams's hands. "Just got off duty. Was heading to my bunk and heard you clowns up here."

"Glad you came, Sergeant," Williams said, happy to engage him in light conversation as his comrades listened noncommittally, tired from their long day of training.

Briggs nodded, turning the beer in his hand. He narrowed

his eyes, as if he were squinting against the rays of the sun, as he looked at the Marines around the room. His brown hair was cut just like the rest of them, but he had a slight hint of gray starting to show along his temples, premature for his twenty-three years. Perhaps it was from the trauma of being in combat—real combat, combat that most of these young Marines who hadn't served a tour overseas only dreamed of, or perhaps feared.

They have no idea, Briggs thought as he scanned the room, touching each of them with his eyes. *They may never see me again, and I don't even get to say good-bye to them. Well, that's typical Marine Corps for you. They give you a medal, orders to leave immediately, and duty on your last day. Typical.* This was a sorrowful, heartbreaking good-bye that he could not even share. *Check, you bastard, what have you gotten me into?* A lump formed in his throat.

"Glad to be here," Briggs said with mock sarcasm. For a moment, the ocean blue in his eyes flashed, eyes which were surrounded by scars, one on each side and a single one underneath his left eye.

"We're about six beers in, so you got some catchin' up to do," said Williams, and a few of the others nodded and lifted their cans in salute, tossing back another gulp.

"Hey, Sergeant, you ever kill anyone?" Butler asked with the slur of several beers dragging through his lips.

"You don't drink much, do you, Butt?" Briggs's response came back with a snap in his voice.

Butler shook his head, then looked down. "Shit." The insensitivity of what he'd asked started to sink in.

Briggs's reputation was well known, and he was somewhat admired and feared by the younger troops. They knew he had killed before. The rumors of how he had killed a man with his bare hands in combat were constantly whispered among the ranks.

"Good night," Briggs said as he passed back the unopened

beer and turned to leave. With no expression and no explanation, he disappeared down the barrack's gangway.

"Yes, I remember my first," Briggs mumbled to himself as he closed the door to his barrack's room behind him. He reached down into his pocket and caressed the Silver Star that he had removed from his uniform. He did not want to explain to the room of young Marines how he came by it, especially knowing that he would be leaving them behind to fight on without him. He laid it on the rack next to the red binder that held the citation and, for a brief moment, attempted to reassure himself that they would be fine without him. But he was not convinced.

He turned on the light, the TV, the light at the end of the hall, and finally the light in the head. There weren't enough light switches in the room to flood out the horrible memory that was welling up inside his body, about to drive him to his knees and torture him once more for a sin he committed in the name of duty, honor, and the Corps.

"Oh God, here it comes." Briggs closed the door to the head and sat in the far back corner of the shower stall. Slowly and calmly, he tried to stop the knot from tightening in his stomach. Too strong, too powerful, this damn memory was just too much. "Please God, make it go away, make it leave me alone. Please stop . . ."

But he knew there was nothing that could stop this.

The tears were falling now. Briggs wasn't sure what made him sicker: the horror of what he was capable of doing with the hands that God and his mother gave him, or the body-wracking sobs that came forth to overwhelm him each time. The memory was coming like a freight train on rails. Briggs took several short, choppy breaths, and then one deep breath. He repeated this several times, and each time, he would lift his head and bang it against the tile wall inside the shower stall. It was over.

"Okay, okay. I'm better, much better now," Briggs mumbled as he collected his thoughts. He placed one hand on the floor and pushed himself up on one knee. Placing his right foot firmly on the floor, he pushed up and gripped the wall. He leaned his face against the tile of the shower stall, allowing the coolness of it to linger on his skin. "Much better."

Placing both hands on the sink, he leaned forward and prepared himself for what he was about to see in the mirror. His reflection stared back, tattered and broken and disheveled.

In thirty minutes, the oncoming relief would assume the duty watch. He used this time to pull himself together, to be normal again. Then he washed his face, shed his short-sleeved Charlies, and traded them for comfortable shorts and a Big Rock fishing tournament T-shirt.

When the oncoming relief arrived, he handed him the logbook and the duty roster and left.

As he walked through the door on the way to the parking lot, carrying a small bag with his uniform folded neatly inside, the citation, and the blue jewelry box that held his Silver Star, he felt like he was leaving behind a trail of breadcrumbs for the very last time, leading away from the agony of his memories. It was a two-hour drive back to his mother's house on the Outer Banks, and to Anita. Thoughts bounced around inside his head the entire time, wondering what was next.

He started his car and and sat for just a moment looking straight forward with both his hands on the wheel, lost in the reality of what was going to happen to him when he drove through the gate for what could be the last time. He then unzipped his bag, rifled around inside of it and removed the jewelry box, placing it between him and the steering wheel. He swung his head from side to side, looking through the windows and his mirrors to make sure no one was watching him. Then he opened it and the metal spring that hinged the lid strained as it revealed the shimmering gold star with a smaller silver star at its center. He did this to reassure himself that it was true—a validation of what had happened to him and not part of a shadowy nightmare.

CHAPTER TWENTY-THREE

November 2006

Scott stepped out of the house after retrieving the last two bottles of beer from the refrigerator. It was uncommonly warm for November, but that was typical untypical North Carolina weather. One day it could be freezing cold and the next shorts and T-shirts were the only thing required to make it through the day. And this day was perfect. Temperatures were in the mid-70s and a refreshing breeze blew across the bay between Harkers Island and Gloucester. He was attempting to close the sliding glass door with his hip when his mother entered the kitchen.

"Here, I'll get that for you honey," she said. She stepped in front of him, blocking his path to the backyard.

"You know, you will have to tell her one day. You do know that, don't you, Scott?" his mother said as she reached up and brushed her hand through his hair. Her smile was gentle.

"Tell her what?" Scott asked, surprised. He searched his mother's eyes.

"That you have a new role with the military," she said with knowing eyes. "Oh now, don't look at me as if you have no idea what I am saying. I am your mother, and there are things you will never be able to hide from me. A mother knows, Scott, just like a wife knows. I knew all about your father's work with the Service, and I know you are doing the same thing. You can't hide it from her." His mother nodded her head at Anita, who was sitting at the end of the pier.

Scott stared at his mother and held back the urge to ask her some of the many questions he had about his father's past.

"Your father couldn't hide it from me. When you truly love someone, you share a connection that is unspoken and has no boundaries and no secrets. There are some things men don't and will never understand about women. The foundation of the world is built upon the moral shoulders of mothers. When battles rage and politics are enforced by warriors who suffer and fall, somewhere a mother worries, and her burden is great. I watched your father die as a warrior, fighting for a cause that he believed in."

Scott hadn't moved an inch, but his mother didn't seem to notice as she continued.

"Some part of him did it for the money he thought we needed. But the truth is, we would have been just as happy with less and still would have managed to get by." She paused and lightly touched his cheek with her fingers. "You are a lot like your father in many ways—proud, strong, and strong-willed—and if you are as smart as he was, you will choose a strong woman who loves you and can give you good advice, even when you don't want it or think you need it. You and Anita share that kind of love. You and she have waited for one another a long time, and now it is time for that love to blossom on a foundation of honesty." She placed her arm around his shoulders and turned him toward the dock where Anita was waiting.

Anita sat at the far end, her legs hanging over the pier. It was high tide, and her feet were barely touching the crystal-clear, emerald-green water. She was watching the sun submerge itself into the cool waters on the horizon and drawing circles with her toes that quickly faded away. Sweetie was running across the lush green yard that separated the back of the house from the pier. She ran up to Scott and pulled on his pants leg.

"Come on, Mr. Scott, you're missing the sun taking a bath. Hurry," she urged as she pulled with all her might in an effort to hasten him along. Scott stood frozen in his tracks. He turned back to look at his mother.

"She has been waiting for you. She has always been waiting for you, and even though her path was different from the one you took, she is still waiting. And now those two paths have crossed again, just like you knew they would. So go on, Scott. Your family is waiting for you. You and I will have all the time in the world to talk about your father and such things. Hurry up now. Each sunset is a blessing, especially when you share it with people you love."

Scott reached around his mother's neck and gave her a hug, careful not to clang the two beer bottles together.

"I love you, Mom," he said as he gently kissed her on her cheek. He then gave into Sweetie's prodding and pulling and ran alongside her as she raced for the steps to the pier. Scott slowed his pace so that he could take in the vision of the sunset and Anita silhouetted against the brilliant orange light that was now fading into the water's edge, flanked by the marshes and islands.

CHAPTER TWENTY-FOUR

November 2006

"Alpha, this is Tide, over."

Trust reached over and activated his video screen in his private office aboard the *Sereniteit*. "This is Alpha, activate your video transmit now, Tide, over," Trust responded as he leaned back in his black, leather desk chair and took a drag of a large cigar.

On the other end of the radio, a highly trained sniper, one of many in Trust's arsenal of hired killers, lay just inside the wood line on Brown's Island with his weapon trained on Briggs as he walked down the dock. The range was just over eight hundred yards, an easy shot with the wind at his back and the sun setting to his far left. He activated the video feed that booted into his scope and called back to Trust. "You are patched in now, say receive."

"Receive. I have a clear visual," Trust replied as he picked up an oversized, short-stemmed glass of brandy and swirled it about, allowing the aroma to fill his nostrils before he took a small sip and placed it back on his desk.

"Waiting," Tide replied as he slowed his breathing and relaxed his heart rate. His thumb was poised on the safety, his thoughts clear. He waited comfortably, perched behind the scope of his heavy barreled M-40 rifle. The oversized silencer poked out several inches past the folding stabilizer legs mounted at the end of the stock. The shot would be deadly and its sound unheard.

Trust, too, waited as he sat in his position of power, totally in control and watching Briggs as he sat down next to Anita and placed Sweetie on his lap. He passed Anita a beer with a sliver of lime tucked inside the neck of the bottle, leaned over, and kissed her, then turned his attention toward the setting sun. Trust had a front row seat with the best view possible as he read Briggs's lips. *I love you.* The only obstruction was the fine crosshairs of the riflescope.

He knew if he told Tide to shoot, the next thing he would see would be the little girl's chest explode—Tide would not hesitate to shoot through her in order to take out his objective. He would then swing the scope slightly to his right and deliver another round to silence the only witness. There was no extra money for killing three instead of one; however, Tide would know it would buy him at least forty-five minutes of time, valuable time he would use to put distance between himself and a job accomplished.

Trust paused and took another drag from his cigar. He marveled at the steadiness of the image before him; Tide's aim never changed, and the scope's view barely wavered more than an inch from the top button on the little girl's sweater, just in front of Briggs's heart.

This was the kind of power Shelby Trust craved—a life at his whim.

Trust reclined in his desk chair as far back as it would go. The leather along with the two mounting springs at its base creaked in unison. He swirled the oversized glass of brandy and buried his nose into it so deep that the edge of the glass touched his forehead. He inhaled the intoxicating liquor. But the euphoria he was feeling did not come from the glass, it was from the image on the screen in front of him.

"What to do? What to do? What shall I do with you?" Trust quietly whispered to himself, knowing that if he spoke too loudly, Tide might misconstrue his words and send the round to its mark.

Just then, his phone vibrated in his pocket. He removed it from the inside of his dinner jacket liner and held it out far enough from his face so he could see it without using his reading glasses. "Oh," he said as he simultaneously hit the mute button on his radio transmitter to Tide. He put on his reading glasses to verify the number.

"Well, I'll be," he remarked as he sat up straight in his chair and accepted the call. "It's been a long time," he said with a hint of friendship and an overtone of surprise. "I see you still have a flair for nostalgia. You called from our old phone. It is so good to hear from you."

Trust stood and started pacing about his office. He finally came to rest at the corner of his desk as the conversation came to a conclusion. "I will get in touch with you tomorrow. Yes, I understand. Go ahead and make the arrangements. And it is good to hear from you, my friend."

Trust sat back in his chair and reactivated the audio on his computer so Tide could hear him.

"Stand down, Tide. Stand down and verify, over."

"Roger, I verify. Stand down," Tide replied as he cleared his weapon and started gathering up his gear to return to Morehead and wait for his next instructions. Shot or no shot, he would still be paid the same. His purpose was over, for now.

Trust cut off the screen and retrieved his glass of brandy so that he might attend to his guests topside. He glanced at the screen, now blank.

"Not today, Scott. I don't think I will kill you today. You and I have much more to do together." He slowly closed the door to his office and activated the alarm.

The End of Book One